"You

"I answered, "whatever you've got to do."

Mickelbury took off his jacket and tossed it away, revealing the bright red and yellow vest.

"I hope the vest doesn't blind you," he said.

"No you don't," Clint said.

Mickelbury laughed, then moved. He was incredibly fast. His gun cleared leather as Clint pulled the trigger. Clint's bullet went right through the yellow flower on Mickelbury's heart. More red blossomed. Mickelbury had a shocked look on his face. His gun dropped from his hand and he looked down at his chest. With both hands he felt his chest until he found the blood.

"Sonofa—" he started, and then fell facedown in the sand.

DON'T MISS THESE
ALL-ACTION WESTERN SERIES
FROM THE BERKLEY PUBLISHING GROUP

THE GUNSMITH by J. R. Roberts
Clint Adams was a legend among lawmen, outlaws, and ladies. They called him . . . the Gunsmith.

LONGARM by Tabor Evans
The popular long-running series about Deputy U.S. Marshal Custis Long—his life, his loves, his fight for justice.

SLOCUM by Jake Logan
Today's longest-running action Western. John Slocum rides a deadly trail of hot blood and cold steel.

BUSHWHACKERS by B. J. Lanagan
An action-packed series by the creators of Longarm! The rousing adventures of the most brutal gang of cutthroats ever assembled—Quantrill's Raiders.

DIAMONDBACK by Guy Brewer
Dex Yancey is Diamondback, a Southern gentleman turned con man when his brother cheats him out of the family fortune. Ladies love him. Gamblers hate him. But nobody pulls one over on Dex . . .

WILDGUN by Jack Hanson
The blazing adventures of mountain man Will Barlow—from the creators of Longarm!

TEXAS TRACKER by Tom Calhoun
J.T. Law: the most relentless—and dangerous—manhunter in all Texas. Where sheriffs and posses fail, he's the best man to bring in the most vicious outlaws—for a price.

CHICAGO CONFIDENTIAL

J. R. ROBERTS

JOVE BOOKS, NEW YORK

THE BERKLEY PUBLISHING GROUP
Published by the Penguin Group
Penguin Group (USA) Inc.
375 Hudson Street, New York, New York 10014, USA
Penguin Group (Canada), 90 Eglinton Avenue East, Suite 700, Toronto, Ontario M4P 2Y3, Canada
(a division of Pearson Penguin Canada Inc.)
Penguin Books Ltd., 80 Strand, London WC2R 0RL, England
Penguin Group Ireland, 25 St. Stephen's Green, Dublin 2, Ireland (a division of Penguin Books Ltd.)
Penguin Group (Australia), 250 Camberwell Road, Camberwell, Victoria 3124, Australia
(a division of Pearson Australia Group Pty. Ltd.)
Penguin Books India Pvt. Ltd., 11 Community Centre, Panchsheel Park, New Delhi—110 017, India
Penguin Group (NZ), 67 Apollo Drive, Rosedale, North Shore 0632, New Zealand
(a division of Pearson New Zealand Ltd.)
Penguin Books (South Africa) (Pty.) Ltd., 24 Sturdee Avenue, Rosebank, Johannesburg 2196,
South Africa

Penguin Books Ltd., Registered Offices: 80 Strand, London WC2R 0RL, England

This is a work of fiction. Names, characters, places, and incidents either are the product of the author's imagination or are used fictitiously, and any resemblance to actual persons, living or dead, business establishments, events, or locales is entirely coincidental.

CHICAGO CONFIDENTIAL

A Jove Book / published by arrangement with the author

PRINTING HISTORY
Jove edition / November 2010

Copyright © 2010 by Robert J. Randisi.
Cover illustration by Sergio Giovine.

All rights reserved.
No part of this book may be reproduced, scanned, or distributed in any printed or electronic form without permission. Please do not participate in or encourage piracy of copyrighted materials in violation of the author's rights. Purchase only authorized editions.
For information, address: The Berkley Publishing Group,
a division of Penguin Group (USA) Inc.,
375 Hudson Street, New York, New York 10014.

ISBN: 978-0-515-14859-6

JOVE®
Jove Books are published by The Berkley Publishing Group,
a division of Penguin Group (USA) Inc.,
375 Hudson Street, New York, New York 10014.
JOVE® is a registered trademark of Penguin Group (USA) Inc.
The "J" design is a trademark of Penguin Group (USA) Inc.

PRINTED IN THE UNITED STATES OF AMERICA

10 9 8 7 6 5 4 3 2 1

If you purchased this book without a cover, you should be aware that this book is stolen property. It was reported as "unsold and destroyed" to the publisher, and neither the author nor the publisher has received any payment for this "stripped book."

ONE

It had been a while since Clint Adams had been in Chicago just for pleasure.

As always, each time he took a cab from Chicago's Union Station on Canal Street to his hotel—this time on Michigan Avenue—he was struck by how much the city had grown since his last visit. He'd only seen taller buildings on his last trip to New York.

His investments all over the West—mostly saloons and gambling halls, with an occasional piece of a successful ranch—as well as his own profits from poker enabled him to stay in fairly high-class hotels whenever he visited cities like Chicago, Denver, San Francisco, and New York. He felt there was no point in visiting the burgeoning cities if he had to scrimp and save money. It was only when he felt flush enough that he made these trips.

When he got to his hotel he entered the lobby carrying a carpetbag. His gun and holster was inside, but he had his Colt New Line stuck in his belt where nobody could see it—the small of his back.

He registered, got a regular room because he didn't feel the need for suite. He may have been flush, but he wasn't that flush.

"Are you here for business or pleasure, sir?" the clerk asked. He was well dressed and chipper, just trying to do his job and be cheerful and helpful at the same time.

"Pleasure," Clint said, "purely pleasure."

"Excellent," the man said. He held out a key and said, "Enjoy your stay."

"I intend to."

"Need help with your bag, sir?"

"No, I've got it. Thanks."

"Anything else I can do for you?"

"I'd like a bath."

"When?"

"Right away."

"It'll be waitin' when you come back down, sir."

He took the key and made his way up the stairs to the second floor. He'd been on elevators before and still didn't like them. The stairs were fine with him.

In his room he dropped the bag on the bed and went to the window. East, West or in between, he was always careful. There was a sheer drop outside, so there was no danger of anyone coming in that way. That left only the door, which was heavy, with a good lock on it.

If he'd taken a suite he probably would have had bath facilities in the room. Now for a bath he had to go downstairs and arrange it. That suited him, too. He fished something clean and more casual than his traveling suit out of his bag and went downstairs.

* * *

As Clint went upstairs the clerk grabbed a piece of paper, hastily wrote a note, then called over a bellhop and told him to hand-deliver it.

After his bath, Clint dropped his suit back in his room, then went back downstairs. The hotel was called the Templar, and attached was a saloon called the Bull & Calf. It actually said it was a pub. He knew from a trip to England years ago that they called their saloons and bar public houses.

There was a door leading to the pub from the hotel lobby. He went inside and approached the bar. It was midday and quiet. The bar was burnished brass and mahogany, and most of the customers were wearing suits. In a city like Chicago, it was hard to tell gamblers from bankers; in some ways they were very alike.

"What can I get for you?" the bartender asked.

"Beer, nice and cold."

"Coming up, friend."

When he brought the beer the bartender asked, "Staying at the hotel?"

"Sure am."

"You give me your room number we can put your drinks on your hotel bill. New thing we're trying."

"That sounds dangerous," Clint said. "I think I'll just pay cash."

"That's fine, but the offer still stands. Drinks or food."

"I'll keep it in mind."

"My name's Seamus, if you need anything."

The two men shook hands.

"I thought I detected an Irish accent."

"Been in this country for twenty years, came here

when I was fifteen. The accent is a hard thing to shake. If I ain't workin' it comes back—or if I ain't careful, like now."

"The accent works for me, Seamus," Clint said.

"I thank you kindly, but management don't feel the same."

"Then why call the place the Bull & Calf?" Clint asked. "Seems to me having a bartender with an Irish accent would work in their favor."

"I don't know about that," Seamus said. "All I know is they asked me to tone it down. I need this job, so I try my best."

"Well, you're doing a good job."

Seamus looked down the bar, saw three customers, all occupied by their drinks. Same went for the three or four tables that were taken. He decided he had time to chat, so he leaned his forearm on the bar.

"You look and sound like a Westerner."

"You got me," Clint said. "Just got in on the train."

"Been to Chicago before?"

"Many times, but not for a while."

"It's growin' faster 'n faster," Seamus said, not bothering to try to hide his accent, now. "'Tis a wonder, it is."

"I know," Clint said. "I saw many new buildings just between here and the station."

"What brings you here?"

"Just pleasure," Clint said. "I haven't been here in a while."

"Know anybody in town?"

"A few people."

"Then you don't need no help gettin' around, eh?" Seamus asked.

Clint didn't know if the man was offering him some female companionship or just directions, but he said, "No, I got it all covered."

"Well, that's good, then. 'scuse me, got another customer."

"See you," Clint said.

Seamus moved down the bar. Clint thought about the people he knew in Chicago. He didn't figure to contact any of them on this trip. Most of them were Pinkerton detectives, and he didn't intend to get involved in any of their business this time around.

No, this trip was just for him. He'd even left Eclipse, his Darley Arabian, behind in Labyrinth, Texas, in the capable hands of his friend Rick Hartman. He didn't intend to do anything that would make it necessary for him to get on horseback.

And at that point he wasn't even thinking about what they said about the best-laid plans of mice and men.

But he should have been.

TWO

While Clint was in the Bull & Calf, the bellhop delivered the clerk's handwritten message to a man who was sitting in the restaurant having his supper.

The man, tall, middle-aged, well dressed, read the note and then dismissed the bellhop with a wave of his hand. He then folded the note and tucked it away in his jacket pocket. The waiter came over and set a steaming plate down in front of him.

"There you go, Mr. Bascomb."

"Thank you."

The news was interesting, but did not require immediate attention. Not when there was a perfectly cooked steak on a plate in front of him.

Clint nursed his beer, then had a second, which Seamus assured him was on the house. As it got later more and more people came in. Clint decided to get outside before nightfall and take a walk. He finished his second beer and waved to Seamus, who waved back.

It was a perfect fall evening. The weather wasn't cold enough for a jacket, but he wore one to hide the New Line in the back of his belt.

He walked down Michigan Avenue, looking up at the tall buildings, watching the people go by on the streets. He liked the fact that no one knew who he was, no one except Rick knew where he was, and he wasn't likely to be recognized—not here.

His thoughts turned to food, and rather than return to his hotel he just stopped at a restaurant. One of the things about Chicago was that you could get good food almost anywhere, no matter how the place looked. This one could have used some spit and polish, but the smell that hit him when he entered set his mouth to watering.

"Help you?" a cute waitress asked him.

"Yes," he said, "I'm looking for some good home cooking."

"Doll," she said, "you came to the right place."

Carter Bascomb finished his steak, then left the hotel and flagged down a passing cab. It was an open carriage, which suited him. He liked to feel the wind on his face.

He gave the driver an address on Rush Street and then sat back to enjoy the ride.

THREE

The pot roast Clint ordered was the most tender meat he had ever eaten; he told the waitress so when she came by to check on his meal.

"I'll tell the cook," she said. "He always likes to hear good things about his cookin'. Now how about some dessert? A piece of pie?"

"What kind of pie you got?" he asked.

"You name it," she said. "Apple, cherry, rhubarb—"

"Peach?"

"Oh, yes," she said. "Very good peach."

"I'll have a slice and some coffee."

"Comin' up."

While he was waiting for his dessert he looked around and found that the place had emptied out.

"What's going on?" he asked as she set his pie and coffee in front of him.

"What do you mean?"

"Where'd everybody go?"

"We don't encourage folks to stay after they finish

eating," she answered. "We want other people to come in."

"And they know that?"

"Sure," she said. "Everybody around here knows that."

"I'll be sure to leave when I'm done," he said.

She bumped him with her hip and said, "You can stay around for a while, honey. Don't get that many handsome men in here."

He watched her walk back to the kitchen. He was sure she was exaggerating that hip sway for him, and he made sure he enjoyed every minute of it.

Bascomb got out of the cab at the Rush Street address and paid the driver. He waited until the man drove away before approaching the door he wanted, which was several doors down from the address he'd actually given to the driver.

He had a key and used it on the front door, but when he got to the inner door he had to knock.

"Who is it?" a raspy voice asked.

"Bascomb."

The door was opened by a large, bald man named Slater. Bascomb and Slater hated each other, but they worked for the same man and had to get along. The day one of them lost his job, the two would go at it. But not until then.

"You had meat," Slater said, wrinkling his nose. He didn't eat meat, and could smell it on people.

"A big hunk of it," Bascomb said. When he knew he was coming here, he always made sure he ate enough so that Slater got a noseful.

Slater shook his head and said, "Come on, he's expecting you."

Bascomb wondered why Slater always said that. He never came here unless the Man was expecting him.

Slater led him to a room with double sliding doors. They were closed. Slater knocked, then slid them open.

"Bascomb's here," he said.

"Let him in."

Slater stepped aside. Bascomb knew this was a formality. He knew if he wanted in there was no way Slater could keep him out.

"That's enough, Slater," the Man said. "Close the doors."

"Yes, sir."

Slater backed out, but took the time to wrinkle his nose one more time before sliding the doors closed.

"Why do you do that?" the Man asked from behind his desk.

"Do what?" Bascomb asked.

"Eat meat before you come here," the Man said. "You know he hates it."

"That's why I do it."

The Man shook his head.

"Sometimes I think I should fire one of you so I can sit back and have a ringside seat for what comes next," he said.

"Why don't you?"

"Maybe I will," the Man said, "as soon as I figure out which one of you I can most do without. What have you got for me?"

"Not much," Bascomb said. "Got word from the Templar that they have a special guest."

"Who?"

"Clint Adams."

The Man's face was impassive.

"Do you know who—"

"Of course I know who he is," the Man said, cutting Bascomb off. "I'm wondering what he's doing here, and what I can possibly use him for."

Bascomb stood quietly.

"Pour two glasses of brandy, Carter, and give me some time to think."

"Yes, sir."

Bascomb poured two glasses, set one in front of the Man, then sat across from him and waited.

FOUR

Clint found the pie and coffee as good as the steak. The waitress continued to be cute, but the longer he spoke to her, the older he realized she was. He finally decided she was in her early thirties, when upon first glance he'd guessed her ten years younger.

Her name was Marnie, and when he was paying the bill she asked him where he was staying.

"What makes you think I'm not local?" he asked.

"Lots of things," she said. "The way you talk and act, but mostly, you've never been in here before."

"Well, you're right," he said. "I'm staying at the Templar."

"Wow," she said, "fancy. Why aren't you eating there?"

"I was out for a walk and saw your place," he said. "Decided to try it. This is my first day in town. I have plenty of time to eat at my hotel."

"Well, the food's really good there," she said.

"Better than here?"

She smiled.

"I'll let you find that out for yourself," she said. "Let's just say I think you'll be back. What's your name?"

"My name is Clint," he said, "and I think you're right, Marnie. I will be back."

Back at his hotel, he decided one more beer at the Bull & Calf was in order. The place was fairly empty. He approached the bar and Seamus met him there with a beer.

"How did you know?"

"You looked like a man in search of a beer," the Irishman said.

"Where is everybody?" he asked.

"Been and gone," Seamus said. "It's the middle of the week. Most of my clientele has to go to work tomorrow."

"I see."

"Where did you get off to?"

"Went for a walk, had something to eat."

"Where?"

"A little place a few blocks from here."

"That covers a lot of places."

"Well, I didn't get the name, but the steak was good, and so was the pie."

"There's a lot of good food in Chicago," Seamus said. "But if you're ever lookin' for some good Irish food, let me direct you to the place to go."

"I'll keep that in mind, Seamus," Clint said. He finished his beer. "Thanks. I'll see you tomorrow."

"Good night."

Clint left the saloon, crossed the lobby floor, and went up the stairs. All the while he was watched by the desk clerk and knew it. He hoped that the man was just curious.

"Keep an eye on him," the Man said.

Bascomb had been staring into his brandy glass. He was startled by the Man's voice, then by the content.

"Is that all?"

"Yes," the Man said. "I want to know what he does, where he goes, who he sees, before I decide if I can use him."

"And what if he simply leaves town in a couple of days?" Bascomb asked.

"Then we couldn't have used him, anyway," the Man said. "I only need him if he's going to stay."

"Then I should find out how long he's staying," Bascomb said.

"You could do that," the Man said. "If you can do it discreetly."

Bascomb stood up.

"Discreet is my middle name."

"Just don't let him catch on."

"I won't."

"Come back in two days, or before, if you know something," the Man said.

"I will."

Bascomb left the room and made his way back to the front door, where he found Slater waiting.

"That didn't take long," he said. "Guess you didn't get fired."

"Not even close."

"Too bad."

Bascomb turned to face Slater, who was several inches taller—and wider—than he was.

"Are you still sure of yourself?" Bascomb asked.

"Totally."

"There's a lot more involved than height and bulk, you know."

"I know," Slater said.

"Oh well," Bascomb said. "The day will come."

"I can't wait," the larger man said.

"Be patient, Slater," Bascomb said, opening the door. "No one should be in a hurry to die."

Slater walked back to his boss's office and knocked on the door.

"Come."

He entered.

"He gone?" the Man asked, without looking up from his desk.

"Yes sir."

Slater waited for the Man to say something else.

"Sir?"

"Yes?" Still didn't look up from his paperwork.

"What are you gonna do?"

"About what?"

"Adams," Slater said. "Clint Adams."

"Not sure yet, Slater," the Man said, "but there's got to be some use for him."

"He could kill the others," Slater said. "I mean, he is a gun for hire, right?"

The Man sighed and looked up at Slater.

"Let's see what Bascomb finds out," he said. "Then I'll decide."

"When are you gonna let me kill Bascomb?" Slater asked.

"As soon as I'm done with him," the Man said. "As soon as he can't do me any more good."

Slater nodded. It never occurred to him that the Man might feel the same way about him, too.

"That's all, Slater."

"Yes, sir."

"And close the door behind you."

"Yes, sir."

Slater left the office.

As the door closed on Slater, the Man looked up again. Whatever the Gunsmith was doing in Chicago, his presence in town could only be seen as fortuitous. And the Man intended to make good use of him. Eventually, he'd have Bascomb bring Adams to him, and he'd make the Gunsmith an offer the legend couldn't possibly refuse.

That was the only kind of offer the Man ever made to anyone.

FIVE

Clint woke the next morning with the sun streaming through his window, right in his face. He didn't mind it. He was ready to rise, anyway.

He dressed, decided he should seek out a clothing store to reinforce his wardrobe. Funny, he never even thought about the word *wardrobe* unless he was in a large city.

The Templar was an old hotel that had been upgraded to meet with the needs of a new generation. However, since he had one of the older rooms, he still needed to use a pitcher and basin in order to wash before dressing.

Once he hit the lobby, he walked to the entrance of the dining room. Breakfast would be the first meal he had there, but it would still give him an opportunity to compare food.

His server was a waiter in his sixties, with a bald head and a bow tie. Marnie's little restaurant was already ahead in the comparison.

"Steak and eggs," he ordered. "And a pot of strong coffee."

"Yes, sir."

"And some biscuits."

"Coming up, sir."

He studied his fellow diners while he waited. The room was almost full. Every table was occupied, but not every seat.

When the waiter brought his meal, he asked, "Are you a guest in the hotel, sir?"

"Yes, but I'll be paying cash for my meals."

"As you wish, sir."

After his first bite, Clint decided the small restaurant from the night before had a better cook—at least on this day. But the meal was palatable, and he enjoyed it.

Bascomb sat across the dining room from Clint, working on his own breakfast. He had been nursing it for half an hour, and the contents had begun to congeal on his plate. He poured himself another cup of coffee and watched the famous Gunsmith eat.

For a living legend, he looked rather ordinary to Bascomb. He didn't even seem aware of his surroundings.

Bascomb made sure to be discreet as he watched Clint Adams. He wasn't ready for the man to see him. Perhaps later, in a saloon, he'd make the legend's acquaintance.

Clint had a sixth sense that told him whenever he was being watched. It had been acquired over the course of many years, and he never ignored it. But he couldn't pick anybody out. Whoever was watching him was very good at it. However, he made a thorough sweep of the room, committing their faces to memory. If someone was interested in him, eventually they'd make contact. And when that time came, he'd remember the face.

He continued to eat his breakfast. He was able to commit the faces to memory without looking like he was actually doing it.

By the end his meal, he was satisfied that if any of these people approached him, he'd know it.

"Was everything satisfactory, sir?" the waiter asked.

"Oh yes," Clint said. "Very good. Thanks."

"Excellent, sir," the waiter said. "I hope we'll be seeing you again."

"I'm sure you will."

Clint spent the day at a couple of museums, had lunch in a small café that allowed him to sit outside, and watched all the pretty women as they walked by.

He was being followed. He could feel it, but couldn't spot it. He was impressed that somebody from the fifty could watch him, and follow him without being spotted.

He was going to be very interested in whoever it was, when he was finally approached.

Carter Bascomb watched Clint Adams all day. Museums, parks, restaurant. What the hell was he up to? Could it be the man was really there just to relax? Maybe get away from all the killing he did in the West?

Bascomb was getting bored. He decided not to spend another day watching him. Tonight he'd make contact with Adams and find out what was going on.

What was Clint Adams doing in Chicago?

SIX

Clint decided to finish his day up by paying another visit to Marnie. The lunch he'd had didn't compare with the food she'd served him, or even with what he'd had for breakfast. He wanted a supper he knew he'd enjoy, so he went back to that small restaurant.

"You came back," she said, greeting him at the door.

"You said I would," he said. "I didn't want to make a liar out of you."

"Take any table," she said. "Want to start with coffee?"

"And a steak dinner," Clint said.

"Ooh, serious business," she said. "You really want to test our food, huh? Okay, steak it is."

He took a seat and looked around, wondering if the person who'd been watching him all day was there. There were only a few tables occupied: a husband and wife, two women, and a man. But they had all been there when he got there. There was no way his watcher could have known he was coming here, so he discounted them all.

Maybe the next person who walked in would be the one.

Bascomb stopped across the street from the restaurant. He could see that there were few diners inside. If he walked in there now, he'd probably give himself away. He had to wait. Maybe back at the hotel Adams would stop in at the bar.

That would be perfect.

The steak put the one he had for breakfast to shame. The vegetables, the onions, it was all beyond belief.

"What, you're surprised?" Marnie asked, reading the look on his face.

"There's a lot of good food in Chicago," he said. "I know that, but this . . . who's the cook?"

"What makes you think I'm not the cook, huh?" she asked, standing hip shot, her head titled to the other side.

"I don't think you could be out here and in there at the same time," Clint said.

"Well, you're right," she said. "The cook's my brother."

"Your brother?"

"What can I say?" she asked. "He's just a better cook than I am, so he works the kitchen and I work out here. Believe me, you wouldn't want him serving you his food. He's not as cute as I am."

"I can believe that," he said. "You're the cutest thing I've seen since I arrived in Chicago—and I've been to museums."

"Museums," she said. "I'm impressed."

It was later than it had been the night before when he was there. More people started coming in: couples, families, two businessmen. But he disregarded them. Whoever it was, he—and he'd already decided it was a *he*—was a professional. He'd know that he'd give himself away by walking in here.

Clint had to wonder how a professional had discovered that he was in town. There was only one way: Somebody at the hotel had to have given him up.

It was getting dark outside. He wasn't seated near a window, but he could across the street to several darkened doorways. He stared, but there was no movement.

If his watcher was there, he was better than good at what he did.

"Say, Marnie, is there a back way out of here?"

"No. Why, you gonna run out on your bill?"

"No," he said. "I think I have somebody following me."

"Following you?" she asked. "An admirer?"

"I doubt it."

"Do they want to rob you?"

"I'm not sure," he said. "All I know right now is that they're watching me."

"Are you serious?"

"Dead serious."

"Why? Are you somebody important?"

"Not so you'd notice."

"Well, eat your food before it gets cold," she said. "Maybe you can hang around here 'til we close and I'll get you out."

"When do you close?"

"Around ten."

"And what will I do here until then?"

"I don't know," she said with a shrug. "We're gonna have a lot of dishes to wash."

SEVEN

Bascomb was starting to get suspicious.

Many of the diners who had gone in before him had come out. Adams had to be finished eating by now. What else could he be doing in there? Was there a back door? Had Adams spotted him and gone out a different exit?

Or was he still in there, waiting?

But waiting for what?

Clint was up to his elbows in hot water.

"You do that well," Marnie said.

"I've washed dishes before."

She smiled. Beyond her he could see her brother, cleaning his stove now that they were finished serving. She'd taken Clint into the kitchen and introduced him to her brother, Matthew. Only Matthew didn't say a word.

"He doesn't talk much," she told him. "Don't take it personal."

"I'll try not to."

Every so often, Matthew would look over at him.

Marnie was right: He wasn't as cute as she was. In fact, he was downright ugly. It was hard to believe they were brother and sister. She was about five four, while he towered over her by maybe a full foot. She had finely sculpted features, while his were blunt and almost malformed. No wonder he stayed in the kitchen.

He finished washing dishes and dried his hands and arms. Marnie had finished cleaning off the tables, and Matthew was done with the stove.

"So where do you go now?" Clint asked. "You and Matthew?"

"We go home," she said.

"Where's home?"

"Through that door," she said, pointing to an old-looking door almost behind the stove, which he hadn't seen until now.

"You said there was no back door."

"There isn't," she said. "That door leads upstairs, where we live. You want to come up?"

"As long as Matthew doesn't mind," he said.

"Matthew will just go to his room, like he always does," she said. "We'll have the rest of the place to ourselves."

He wondered if that meant what it sounded like?

When the lights went out in the restaurant, Bascomb thought that was it. But he didn't leave right away. He wanted a few moments, and he was rewarded when a light went on in an upstairs window. Apparently the people who owned the place lived upstairs. But did that mean Adams was up there with them?

Bascomb left his hiding place and crossed the street. He had to walk a few buildings down before he found an alley, which he followed to the back of the buildings. From there, he was able to work his way over to the back of the restaurant. When he got there he saw that there was no back door.

Adams was either upstairs, or he'd gone out a window. The only reason he'd have to go out a window would be if he'd spotted his tail, and Bascomb knew that was impossible. He was too good to be spotted.

It had to be an instinct that told Adams that something was wrong.

Bascomb retraced his steps and once again took up a position across the street. He'd give it a little while longer before returning to the hotel to see if Adams was there.

When they reached the second floor, Marnie said goodnight to her brother, who went to his room. That left Clint alone with her in the living room.

"You can stay here for a little while, if you think it will help," she said.

"I'm not sure."

He walked to the front window and tried to peer out the window without moving the curtain too much. The doorways across the street were pitch-black.

"Whoever it is, he's good," he said.

"How do you know it's a he?"

"It's a feeling I have," he said, stepping away from the window and turning to face her.

"We have a kitchen up here," she said. "Would you like something? Coffee? Tea?"

"No, thanks," he said. "I'm still full from that great supper."

"How about something stronger?"

"No, thanks."

"Well," she said, moving closer to him. The bodice of her dress was just low enough to show a little cleavage, but what it showed was dark and mysterious. "What else can I offer you?"

"Marnie—"

"My room is over here," she said, pointing to a doorway. "I'm going to go and change into something else."

She walked to her doorway, then turned and said, "Make yourself at home."

EIGHT

Clint wasn't sure what he was supposed to do.

Did she want him to follow her, after giving her some time to change?

How would she feel if he just left? Insulted?

And if he did follow her, what about her brother, in another room across the way?

He went back to the window and looked out, staring long and hard at the darkened doorways. At one point he thought there was movement in one of the doorways, but he couldn't be sure.

He knew he wasn't imagining being watched, being followed, but could it have been someone following him, with no knowledge of who he was? Maybe they picked him up at his hotel and figured anyone who could afford to stay there was worth robbing?

"Tell me about yourself, Clint," Marnie said, coming back into the room.

He turned and stopped short. She was wearing a filmy-looking robe, with something just as filmy beneath it.

The result was very interesting. There were hints of flesh in the double film. She'd also washed and applied a scent, probably trying to get rid of the fried-food smell from working in the restaurant all day.

"Well," he said, "for one thing my name is Clint Adams."

She stared at him, apparently completely clueless, and he believed her.

"Should I know the name?" she asked. "I'm sorry, but I'm not a student of the . . . what are they calling it now . . . the Old West?"

"That's okay," he said. "It's not important. I have a certain reputation, and whoever's following me might be someone who recognized me. Or it might just be someone who wants to rob me. Who knows?"

"I could send Matthew for a policeman," she said, her tone teasing, "and he could walk you safely home. But if you have a reputation, you probably don't need that. You could probably take care of this man yourself."

"I'm not looking for any trouble while I'm here," he told her. "I've been trying to keep a low profile."

"Well," she said, "like I said, you could stay here for a while . . . an hour . . . all night, if you want." She waved a hand. "That couch is not very comfortable, but my bed is . . . and it's big enough for the two of us."

"But Matthew . . ."

"He won't hear," she said. "When his head hits the pillow, he's out."

She walked over to him, took his hand.

"Don't you think I'm pretty?"

"You know I do."

"Don't you want me?"

"Marnie—"

"Because I want you," she said. "From the first time you came in, and then after you came back . . . well . . . I thought . . ."

She rose onto her toes to kiss him, then, and he gathered her into his arms and kissed her back. She pressed her crotch tightly against him, felt the hardness of him and ground herself against it.

"Mmm," she said, "you do want me . . ."

"Any man would be a fool not to."

"Then come with me," she said, Taking his hand again and tugging him toward the door of her room. "Leave whoever it is out there. Maybe by the time we're done, he'll have gone away."

She pulled him into her room and closed the door behind them.

"Or maybe by morning he'll just get bored," she said, dropping her robe to the floor . . .

Bascomb wondered about going up there, but that would cause a heck of a lot of trouble, and that wasn't what he was after. Not yet, anyway.

The light continued to burn in one window, a window he was sure he had seen Clint Adams peering out of at least once. The man definitely knew that he—or someone—was out here, but Bascomb was still sure he hadn't been spotted all day. Sure Adams had a reputation, but this was Bascomb's town, his back yard, not Adams's.

He had to maintain his anonymity for the moment, as the Man wanted him to be discreet. In the end, he decided to walk back to the hotel and wait there in the Bull & Calf. Maybe Adams would stop in for a drink before he turned in. If so, Bascomb could meet him, maybe buy the man a drink, and find out what he was doing in town.

Bascomb had noticed the pretty waitress in the restaurant. If Adams had gone upstairs with her, then he'd be a couple of hours, at least.

The Bull & Calf was a good place to kill time over some good liquor.

NINE

The filmy gown slid to the floor, right after the robe did, and Marnie was standing there naked. The light from the lamp made her glow. There was downy hair on her arms, and a tangle of gold hair between her legs. She was slender, with small breasts that were like hard peaches, with pink nipples already distended.

"I might still smell a little like fried food—" she started, but he cut her off.

"You smell just fine," he said, "and you're beautiful."

"Thank you," she said. She approached him, started to undo his belt. "Now it's time for me to see you."

She undid the belt and tugged down his pants. He grabbed the Colt New Line from behind his back before it could fall.

"You don't need a gun for me, sir," she assured him.

He reached out, laid the gun on a nearby dresser as she pulled down his shorts. His erection stood out, hard and throbbing, and she said, "Oh my."

"I have to get out of my boots," he said, "or I'll trip on these pants around my ankles."

"Well," she said, smiling, "you just sit on the edge of the bed and we'll take care of that."

She sat him on the bed, removed his boots, his pants, his shorts, then got on her knees in front of him and ran her hands over his thighs.

"It's been a long time for me," she said, staring at his hard cock.

"A pretty girl like you? Why?"

"The local men are afraid of my brother."

"Is he violent?"

"No," she said, "but you've seen him. He's big. And he's not cute."

"Should I be afraid?"

"Oh, no," she said. She took his penis in one hand and stroked it. "No, not at all. But you do have to be afraid of me."

"And why's that?"

She smiled, said, "I may never let you out of this room," and took him in her mouth.

As the heat of her engulfed him, he thought that might not be such a bad thing.

In his room, Matthew was thinking about his sister and the man, Clint. She had never brought a man up to their rooms before. He wondered if she was going to fall in love with him and then leave? She promised she would always take care of him, but what if she fell in love? That's what women did, right? Fell in love?

He rolled over in his bed and covered his ears. Eventually, he fell asleep.

* * *

Marnie wet Clint's cock, sucked it noisily while he ran his hands down her back, slid his finger along the crack between her buttocks.

"We need to get up on this bed," he said.

"You scoot up," she said, releasing him from her mouth, "and I'll crawl on top of you."

He scooted back as he was told and reclined, and as promised she crawled on top of him. Her skin was white-hot, as was her crotch, which she rubbed and down the length of him. Her pubic hair scratched him, creating amazing sensations on his sensitive skin. Then she rubbed hard and began to wet him. Finally, she slid atop him and took him inside of her.

"Sorry," she gasped, "I meant to go slow, but I just can't . . . ooh, yeah . . ."

"You go as fast or slow as you want," he said in her ear.

"Mmmm," she said, eyes closed, riding him up and down, slow—almost painfully slow for him, but he didn't want to ruin it for her. He matched her rhythm, watched her with fascination as she let her head fall back. Then he pulled her down to him so he could kiss her hard breasts and nipples. She held her head to him, stopped moving on him but kept him inside her.

She kissed his mouth, his neck, then his chest, then began moving again, but he felt like it was his turn.

He flipped her over, popping out of her, and she complained, reaching for him. But instead, he slid down between her legs and began to lick and kiss her there.

She caught her breath, stammered, "Oh—oh my—G-God—" Marnie bit her lip as he continued to avidly eat her. He could feel her body tensing, knew she was going to want to scream. But even as she began to buck beneath him, she turned her head and pushed it into the pillow so that whatever cries did escape were muffled.

TEN

"Oh my God," Marnie said, sitting with her back against the wall and her arms crossed, "that's never happened to me before."

"Maybe it's just been so long you don't remember," Clint offered.

"Oh, no," she said, "I'd remember that." She pointed at him. "*That* never happened to me before. Is that supposed to happen?"

"Yeah . . . sometimes . . ." Clint said. "When two people are enjoying each other."

"We were doing that," she said, then she dropped her arms so he could see her breasts, "and I want to do it again."

He crawled over to her and said, "Fine with me," and kissed her. She reached between them and took hold of him as he swelled.

"God, you're already ready to go again?"

"That's only because of you," he said.

"Wait, wait," she said, pushing him away.

"What?"

"I lost control there for a while," she said. "Was I loud? Do you think we woke Matthew?"

"You may think you lost control, but you didn't make a sound," he said. "I was very impressed."

She grinned and said, "Oh, so was I, Mr. Adams. So was I."

She reached for him again.

Bascomb walked back to the hotel, entered the Bull & Calf, got himself a beer and a glass of whiskey, then grabbed a table from where he could see the whole room. He intended to down the whiskey and nurse the beer until Clint Adams showed up. If he didn't appear, then Bascomb knew he'd have to start all over again the next morning.

Or maybe he'd just bring Clint Adams up to see the Man and let him worry about it.

Clint had one of Marnie's ankles in his hand, her leg sticking straight up into the air, as he drove himself into her.

"Ooh," she said, "this is a . . . position I've never been in . . . ahhhh . . . I kinda . . . like it . . . Jesus! I've been missing a lot, haven't I?"

"Shh," he said, "you'll wake your brother."

"Oh God . . ." she said, and bit her lip again.

Clint continued to pound in and out of her, this time concerned with his own pleasure, and not hers. He could feel his release building up inside of him, until finally it was he who had to bite his lip to keep from bellowing as he spurted into her . . .

* * *

"But you could stay all night," she told him a short time later.

"No," he said. "I have to get back to my hotel, and I want to take a look at the street."

He was getting dressed while she watched him from the bed.

"But you'll be coming back, right?"

He went over to the bed to kiss her.

"Sure, I'll be back," he said. "Where else am I going to find a cook as good as your brother?"

She took a swipe from him as he backed away from the bed, laughing, and went out her bedroom door.

Being as quiet as he could, he went to the window to peer out again. Of course, the doorways were still pitch-black, but his instinct told him he had waited out his watcher.

Again, walking softly, he treaded over to the door that led down to the restaurant. He wondered how he was going to lock it behind him. However, once he was outside and pulled the door shut behind him, he realized it had locked on its own.

He stared across the street, and could now see that the darkened doorways were empty. He looked both ways, then looked up, wondering if anyone could be on a rooftop. If whoever was following him wanted to take a shot at him, it would have happened already. No, it was the aim of the watcher to follow and observe. Thinking the tail on Clint might have been lost, the watcher had probably gone back to Clint's hotel in an attempt to pick him up again.

That's where he would find whoever it was, and make contact.

ELEVEN

Clint walked into the Bull & Calf, looked around, and found what he was looking for. It was a face that he had seen in the dining room earlier, when he'd committed all the faces to memory. A man seated alone, with an empty shot glass and a half-full beer mug in front of him, trying for all the world to look like he wasn't watching the door.

Clint walked to the bar and waved at Seamus. The Irish bartender came over with a beer.

"Been out walkin' around again?" Seamus asked.

"Something like that."

"Well, you can see we're kinda empty again," the barman said. "Folks left to go eat and then go home from there."

"Well, I ate and I wanted a drink before I turn in," Clint said. "Also, I'm looking for somebody."

"Who?"

"Somebody who's looking for me, I think."

Seamus leaned both impressive forearms on the bar.

"Nobody asked for ya."

"No," Clint said, "it'd be somebody who's looking for me but won't ask for me."

"Oh, maybe you mean somebody like shot-and-a-beer, over there," Seamus said. "He's good at it, but he's been sittin' there a while waitin' and watching."

"Yeah, he is good," Clint said, "and yeah, that's who I think I'm talking about."

"Well, he's been here over an hour, nursing that same beer."

"Let me have another shot and beer and I'll take them over to him," Clint said.

"Sure," Seamus said, "here ya go. There ain't gonna be any trouble in here, is there?"

"No," Clint said, "we're just going to talk."

Clint picked up the beer mugs with one hand, the shot with the other, and walked over to the man's table. He set the drinks down and the man looked up at him.

"You're good," the man said. "Picked me out, huh?"

"Saw you at breakfast," Clint said. "Mind if I join you?"

"Hey, you bought the drinks," Bascomb said.

Clint sat down, took a sip of his own beer.

"That you on my tail all day?" he asked.

"Yeah, 'fraid so."

"And watching me from across the street from the restaurant?"

"Guilty of that, too."

"Well then, here I am," Clint said. "What's on your mind?"

"I'm just curious what the Gunsmith is doing in Chicago."

"You recognized me?"

"You're kinda famous."

"Yeah, but not in Chicago," Clint said. "I thought I'd have some time to myself here."

"That what you came to town for?" Bascomb asked. "Just to have some time to yourself?"

"That was the plan," Clint said. "Looks like that's not going to happen now—depending on what you want with me."

"I told you," Bascomb said, "I was just wondering what you were doin' in town."

"That's not good enough."

"What do you mean?"

"You're too good at what you do," Clint said. "You're a professional. You wouldn't be following me just out of curiosity."

Bascomb stared at Clint, sipped about half of the new glass of whiskey.

"Yeah, you're right."

"Why don't we start with your name first?" Clint asked. "Since you already know who I am."

"My name is Bascomb," Bascomb said. "Carter Bascomb."

"And what do you do?"

"You guessed it: I'm a professional, like you."

"So what's on your mind?" Clint asked. "Are you looking to make a name for yourself?"

"Adams," Bascomb said, "around here I do have a name for myself, not you."

"Fair enough," Clint said. "This is your town. So why are you following me around?"

"Doin' my job," Bascomb said. "I work for a man who's interested in you."

"Interested in me for what?"

"He doesn't confide in me," Bascomb said. "I was just told to keep an eye on you, see if I could find out why you're here."

"I see," Clint said. "And what's your boss's name."

"Well," Bascomb said, "in Chicago they just call him 'the Man.'"

TWELVE

"'The Man'?" Clint asked. "What does that mean?"

"It means that in this town he's the man, so there's no need to call him anything else."

"But . . . he's got a name, right?"

"Well, sure," Bascomb said, "everybody's got a name."

"So if I wanted to check this out, all I have to do is ask people about somebody called 'the Man?'"

"Exactly," Bascomb said. "Because everybody in Chicago knows him."

Clint sat back in his chair and stared at Bascomb, who had never had to defend his boss's name before.

"Look at it this way," he said. "If we were in the West, it would be enough for you to tell people that you're the Gunsmith. Right?"

"That's right, I guess."

"So, there you go."

Bascomb finished his whiskey and started in on his new beer, pushing the old one away.

"So, are you going to continue to follow me?" Clint asked.

"I don't know," Bascomb said. "I guess if I want to be bored again. You gonna do anything for excitement tomorrow?"

"Not likely."

"Then maybe I should tell my boss," Bascomb said. "He might want to see you."

"What if I don't want to see him?"

"Oh," Bascomb said, "then we might have some trouble." He shrugged. "What would be the harm in talking to him?"

"None, I guess," Clint said. "I guess I'd just like to be invited."

"I'll keep that in mind," Bascomb said. "The wording, I mean."

"Thanks."

"This is a nice place," Bascomb said. "You want another drink?"

"No," Clint said, "I've had enough. I'm going to turn in. I guess I'll be seeing you tomorrow . . . sometime."

"I guess so," Bascomb said. "You know, if you hadn't come over to me I was gonna come over to you."

"I guess that's because we're both professionals," Clint said. "Enjoy the rest of your night."

THIRTEEN

Clint washed up before he went to bed, but when he woke the next morning he could still smell Marnie on him. As he rose and washed again, it occurred to him he hadn't even gotten her last name.

As he dried off, he started thinking about Carter Bascomb and the Man. He assumed the Man was in charge of most of the crime that went on in Chicago, and Bascomb was his right-hand man. If the pair believed most of Clint's reputation, they might have been thinking they could use him, somehow. All he had to do was meet with the Man and tell him no. But considering how he liked to be referred to, this 'Man' was bound to have an ego. He probably didn't take no for an answer.

As he left his room to go downstairs for breakfast, he decided to make contact with one of the people he knew in Chicago.

If anyone knew the story behind the Man, it would be a Pinkerton detective.

* * *

He went to the Pinkerton office and asked for two detectives. Both were out of town on cases. In the end, he simply asked to see Robert Pinkerton, one of old Arthur's sons. Robert and William had been running the agency's various offices since the death of their father.

"Who shall I say is asking to see him?" the secretary asked.

"Tell him it's Clint Adams."

"Clint Adams?" She was young. "Will he know your name?"

"Yes, he'll know my name."

"Just a moment."

She stood up, walked to a door, and went inside. When she came out, she left the door open and stepped aside.

"Mr. Pinkerton will see you now."

"Thank you."

He entered the office. Robert Pinkerton, looking tall, fit, and well-dressed, stood behind his desk.

"Clint Adams," he said. "What's the Gunsmith doing in Chicago?"

"I thought I was relaxing."

The two men shook hands and Pinkerton waved a hand at an empty chair.

"Have a seat and tell me what I can do for you."

"I've only been in Chicago a couple of days and already I've crossed path with somebody named Bascomb, who works for somebody who calls himself—"

"The Man."

"Right."

"And we're talking about Carter Bascomb?"

"Right again."

"Well, you've managed to run across Chicago's new crime boss," Pinkerton said. "How did you do that?"

"You got me," Clint said. "I caught this Bascomb fella following me, and he says his boss told him to do it."

"Why?"

"To see what I was up to," Clint said, "maybe find out why I was in Chicago."

"Which is actually . . . trying to take some time off?"

"Yes."

"From what, exactly?"

"From life."

"Ah."

"So what's this 'Man's' real name?"

"You ready?" Robert asked. "And this is probably why he prefers to call himself the Man."

Clint waited.

"His name is Rodney Hughes."

"Rodney?"

Pinkerton nodded.

"When did he come to town?"

"About a year a half ago, and he's made a big impression."

"And Bascomb?"

"Bascomb is a native Chicagoan," Pinkerton said. "Has a reputation as a hard man, somebody you don't want to tangle with."

"As a killer?"

"Not as such, but he seemed to become aligned with Hughes early on. Oh, and there's another component, a man named Slater."

"What's his claim?"

"He's a big guy who likes to work with his hands," Pinkerton said. "And he's also is a killer."

"Been to prison?"

"Once," Pinkerton said. "Now he's Hughes's, um, well, manservant, I guess you'd call him."

"And Bascomb's the right-hand man?"

Pinkerton nodded and said, "The *Segundo*, as you'd say in the West."

"I see."

"My guess is that Hughes is going to try to recruit you," Pinkerton said. "Probably believes most of your reputation, thinks you're a killer for hire."

"Doesn't he have any of his own?"

"Oh yes, a few—including Slater—but you showing up in his backyard would be a little hard for him to resist."

"Well then," Clint said, "I can listen to his offer and turn him down."

"You probably could get away with that," Pinkerton said. "I wouldn't suggest it to anyone else."

"Why not?"

"He simply doesn't like to be told no."

Clint stood up.

"I'll keep that in mind. Thanks for seeing me, Robert."

"Not at all." Robert stood and they shook hands. "You've done us a good turn or two in the past. Don't see any reason not to return the favor."

Clint left. He agreed there was no reason why they couldn't do each other favors, but he was glad Pinkerton had not invited him to dinner.

FOURTEEN

Bascomb went to see his boss the next morning. He and Slater went through their usual song and dance until he was finally admitted to the inner sanctum.

"He spotted you?" the Man asked.

"No, he didn't. Not really. He picked me out."

"How did he know he was being followed and watched?" the Man asked.

"Instinct."

"He's good, then."

"He's very good," Bascomb said. "That's why he has a reputation."

"Did you tell him anything?" the Man asked.

"Only that you might be wanting to talk to him."

"And what was his reaction?"

"He wasn't against it."

"Did you tell him why?"

"I couldn't," Bascomb said. "I don't know why, do I?"

"No," the Man said, "no, you don't. Well, all right, then."

"All right, what?"

"Bring him here."

"He did tell me one thing."

"What was it?"

"That if he came to see you it would be because he was invited."

"I see." Bascomb watched the Man as his mind worked. His face revealed nothing. "All right, then. Invite the gentleman here."

"Okay."

Bascomb stood up to leave.

"Don't get into it with him, Bascomb," the Man said. "I know how you like a challenge."

"He would be a challenge," Bascomb said, "but I'll wait for you to give the word—*if* you give the word."

"First let's see if I can make any use of him," the Man said.

"Okay."

As he turned to leave, the Man said, "Bascomb, he didn't give you any indication why he was really here?"

"Just to relax, he said."

"Men like that don't relax," the Man said. "Not ever. Don't you agree?"

"Definitely," Bascomb said. "If men like that relax, they die."

"Exactly."

Bascomb waited.

"All right, you can go."

Bascomb nodded and headed for the door again.

"And try not to kill Slater on your way out," the Man said.

"I'll try my best."

* * *

"So you bringin' the Gunsmith here?" Slater asked as they walked to the door.

"I'm going to invite him here," Bascomb said. "Whether or not he comes will be up to him."

"The Man agreed to that?"

"Oh, yes."

"When?" Slater asked. "When will you bring him?"

At the door, Bascomb turned to face the bigger man.

"You sound like a fan, Slater."

"I've read all the books about him and men like him," Slater admitted. "I just want to see if he's really what they say he is."

"I think we're all going to find that out very soon," Bascomb said.

FIFTEEN

When Clint left the offices of the Pinkerton Agency, he considered getting on a train and leaving Chicago. Maybe he should get off in St. Louis and try to relax there instead.

On the other hand, wouldn't that be like getting run out of town by a gangster? Perhaps it would be better to go and have a meeting with the man and see if he could be persuaded to take no for an answer.

If, indeed, he made any kind of offer.

When Clint arrived back at the Templar, he found Carter Bascomb waiting for him in the lobby.

"That didn't take long, did it?" Clint asked.

"Been out . . . relaxing?"

"Actually, I was out trying to get some information on your boss."

"Did you manage to find anyone brave enough to talk about him?"

"Pinkertons aren't usually afraid to talk," Clint said.

"Ah, you know somebody at the Pinkertons?"

"I know a lot of people there," Clint said. He didn't bother saying who he had actually spoken with.

"Well, I'm here with an invitation," Bascomb said. "The Man would like to talk with you. He invited you up to his office."

"Any chance this meeting could take place somewhere else?"

"Like where?"

Clint shrugged. "Someplace public."

"Not a chance," Bascomb said. "If the man goes out in public, somebody will try to kill him. You must know what that's like."

"Actually, I do."

"Do you accept the invitation?"

"Will it involve food?" Clint asked.

"Not likely."

"Why don't I buy you something to eat here in the hotel dining room?" Clint asked. "Then we can go and see him."

"Eat here?" Bascomb said. "Why not?"

"I'd heard that the food here was good, but this is even better than I thought," Bascomb said, a short time later.

It was between breakfast and lunch, so there weren't that many diners. Clint had a steak, even though he'd already eaten breakfast. He actually wanted some time to talk with Bascomb before they went to see his boss.

Bascomb had also ordered a steak, but he got his with eggs.

"I heard you had a reputation before your boss came to town," Clint said.

"That's right," Bascomb said.

"Why join up with him, then?"

"I didn't join up with him," Bascomb said. "I took a job with him."

"But why?"

"Why not? He offered me a lot of money."

"Weren't you making money on your own?" Clint asked.

"I was, but not as much. The Man is a genius. He's figured out ways to make money that I never would have thought of."

"I see. It's about money."

"Isn't it always?"

"Everything isn't about money."

"It is for me," Bascomb said. He ate his last bite and then sat back. "Thanks for the meal."

"You're welcome."

"Shall we go?"

"I'll pay the bill, and then you can lead the way."

"Before we go up," Bascomb said, in front of their destination, "I better tell you about Slater."

"Oh, I heard about him."

"Well, you can't hear about Slater, you have to experience him."

"Is he a friend of yours?"

"No," Bascomb said. "Slater has no friends. We just work for the same man. And one day, one of us is gonna kill the other one."

"Is that a fact?"

"Oh, yes," Bascomb said. "But that's not what I wanted to tell you."

"What is?"

"He's a fan of yours," Bascomb said. "He's read all the dime novels about you."

"Does that mean he wouldn't kill me even if the Man gave him the word?"

"Oh no," Bascomb said, "he'll kill you on the spot."

"Well, knowing that is a little more important to me."

"Let's go up, then."

SIXTEEN

Clint was impressed by the sheer size of the man who opened the door.

"Slater," Bascomb said, "meet Clint Adams."

"Adams," Slater said.

"Slater."

Clint didn't think the man was reacting to him like a fan.

"You got a gun?" Slater asked.

"Yes."

"I'll need it."

"No."

Slater frowned, looked at Bascomb.

"He's the Gunsmith, Slater," Bascomb said. "He can't give up his gun."

"I can't let him go see the boss while he's carryin' a gun."

"He's not going to kill the boss, Slater," Bascomb said. "Besides, I'll be in there."

"I'll have to check with the boss."

"That's fine," Bascomb said. "Let's go."

At the door to the Man's inner sanctum, Bascomb and Clint waited while Slater went inside.

"Yes, yes," the Man said to Slater, "let him in with his gun. He's not going to try to kill me."

"Are you sure?" Slater asked.

The Man opened his top drawer, showed Slater the gun there.

"Bascomb is armed, and you'll be outside the door," he said. "I'll be fine. Let our guest in."

"Yes, sir."

"Let me see your gun," Bascomb said.

Clint showed it to him.

"Kinda small."

"It does the job," Clint said, putting it behind his back again. "I don't want to wear my holster on the streets."

"I've got a cut-down .45 in a shoulder rig."

"Heavy gun."

"I feel naked without it."

"I know how you feel."

The door opened and Slater stepped out. "It's okay."

"Thanks," Clint said.

"But I'll be right outside," the big man added.

"I'll keep that in mind."

"Come on," Bascomb said. "I'll make the introductions."

Once in the room, Clint saw a man seated behind a large cherrywood desk. The room itself was crowded with overstuffed furniture that looked unused, bookshelves full of tomes that looked unread. It was as if the man kept the stuff around for appearances.

But it was not "a" man seated behind the desk, but obviously "the" Man. He wondered what the Man would do if Clint called him by name? In fact, he wondered if Slater and Bascomb knew the real name of their boss.

"Boss, this is Clint Adams," Bascomb said. "Adams... the Man."

Clint extended his hand and the Man shook it firmly. He was younger than Clint would have guessed for a man with his kind of stature. In fact, he might not have even been thirty yet. Both Slater and Bascomb were older than he was.

"I hope you don't mind the affectation," the Man said.

"You have a right to be called whatever you want," Clint said. "In fact, I'm impressed that you know it's an affectation."

"Have a seat."

Clint stood. Bascomb remained standing, just to his right and behind him.

"Can we have Bascomb stand where I can see him?" Clint asked.

"Of course," the Man said. "In fact, Bascomb, why don't you sit down, too."

"Yes, sir."

Bascomb sat down next to Clint.

"I have a gun in my top drawer," the Man said.

"I'd expect you to."

"I just want to be up front with you."

"Fine," Clint said. He took the New Line out and set it on the desk. "There." It was still very much within his reach.

"Well then," the Man said, "we can get started."

"Sure," Clint said, "but get started with what... exactly?"

"I'm sure you've already done some checking on me," the Man said.

"You would have expected me to, right?"

"Of course."

"Then you know about me and what I've become here in Chicago since I arrived."

"I've heard some words we don't exactly use where I come from," Clint said." 'Gangster,' 'crime boss.' "

"They're all true," the Man said. "I rule the crime scene here in Chicago with an iron hand."

"Well," Clint said, "if you're going to rule, that's the way to do it."

"Would you mind telling me why you're in Chicago?" the man asked.

"I just came here to relax."

"As Bascomb said to me not so long ago," the man said, "when a man like you relaxes, he dies."

"That's probably true," Clint said. "Relax is not exactly the right word. I just wanted to... go someplace where I could be by myself, and possibly not be recognized. I'm assuming you heard about me from someone at the hotel. Possibly the clerk."

"I have eyes and ears all over town, as you would expect. So you're really not here on... business?"

"What kind of business would you think I'm here on?" Clint asked.

"Killing."

"Killing is not a business to me..." He almost called the Man "Mr. Hughes." He wondered how much trouble that would have caused.

"But I thought . . . I mean, the Gunsmith's reputation . . ."

"You can't believe everything you read," Clint said, then thought he'd go ahead and try it out. He ended his sentence with, "Mr. Hughes."

SEVENTEEN

Nobody said anything or moved, but it seemed as if everyone in the room had stopped breathing.

"I see whoever you checked me out with is very well informed."

He looked at Bascomb, as if he could tell him who that was.

"Sorry," Bascomb said, "I didn't follow him this morning. He did mention the Pinkertons, though."

"Ah."

"I meant no offense," Clint said. "It is your name, right?"

"It is," Hughes said. "But I don't use it much. What about yours?"

"My name?"

"What do you prefer to be called?"

"I prefer to be called by my name," Clint said. "The Gunsmith is not a name I gave myself. It's one I acquired over the years. I'm kind of stuck with it."

"And the same is true of the reputation?"

"Yes."

"But it's not true?"

"Not by half."

"So you are proficient with your weapon, but you're not a killer."

"That's about the size of it."

"But you have killed men."

"Lots of them," Clint said, "when they've tried to kill me, over the years."

"Never for money?"

"Never."

"That's interesting."

"Is that the kind of offer you were going to make me?" Clint asked. "To kill someone for you?"

"I was going to offer you a job," Hughes said. "To tell you the truth, I don't really know what the job would have entailed, yet. It just seemed to me that your appearance in town was something I could use."

"So you want to use me?"

"That sounds . . . no, I wanted to *make use* of you," Hughes said. "There's a difference."

"The subtlety escapes me, I'm afraid," Clint said.

"I'm sorry," Hughes said, "I'm afraid you're taking offense."

"I'm afraid I am," Clint said.

He reached for his gun. Both of the other men tensed, but all he did was pick it up and tuck it behind his back, into his belt, and then stand up.

"I reject your offer of a job, whatever it might be," he said.

"But you haven't heard my complete offer," Hughes said. "I can pay you—"

"Bascomb and I have already had a conversation about

money," Clint said. "He can tell you how I feel about it."

Hughes stood up. "I'm not used to being walked out on."

"If you intend to have any more meetings with me," Clint said, "get used to it. But if you do intend to talk with me again, don't expect me to come here. You'll have to meet me on neutral ground."

"I don't usually leave my home," Hughes said.

"That's too bad," Clint said, "because I won't be coming back here again."

"You might be back," Hughes said, as Clint headed for the door, "but next time maybe it won't be by invitation."

Clint opened the door, found Slater standing in his way.

"Tell him to move," he said.

There was a moment where nothing happened, then Hughes nodded and Slater stepped aside.

"See our guest to the door, Slater," Hughes said. "Bascomb, you stay."

Clint wondered if he'd gotten Bascomb into trouble.

When they got to the door, Slater said, "I heard what you said in the office."

"Listening at keyholes?" Clint asked.

"It's my job."

"So?"

"Was that true?"

"What?"

"What you said about your reputation." Slater said. "About not believing what was written?"

"It was true."

Slater looked upset.

"B-but . . . why would they write it if it ain't true?"

"To sell newspapers and books," Clint said.

"But, you are the Gunsmith, right?"

"Oh, yes," Clint said. "I am the Gunsmith."

"But you just ain't as special as everybody says?"

"No, Slater," Clint said, "I'm more special than everybody says."

He walked out, leaving Slater looking totally confused.

EIGHTEEN

Clint walked to the corner and caught a cab back to his hotel. During the ride he wondered if he had just made himself a powerful enemy in Chicago.

The Man—Rodney Hughes—glared at Bascomb, who strove to look unconcerned.

"You can't blame me for that," he said.

"Why not?"

"You just told me to bring him here," Bascomb said, "and I did that."

"He treated me with disrespect."

"He doesn't really know who you are," Bascomb said. "Not really."

"Then maybe," the Man said, "I should show him who I am. What do you think, Carter?"

"I think maybe he's somebody to leave alone," Bascomb said after a moment.

"Is that advice, Carter?" the Man demanded. "Are you giving me advice?"

"No, sir," Bascomb said. "I'm just saying . . ."

"You still have contacts in John Callan's camp?"

John Callan was the Man's biggest competitor. An older man and native Chicagoan, he hated Rodney Hughes for coming so far so fast.

"I have a contact," Bascomb said.

"The woman, right?"

"That's right."

The Man rubbed his jaw with his hand, then said, "Okay, find out if Callan's got anything going with Adams."

"You think he came here to work for Callan?"

The Man stared at Bascomb.

"Damn it, that's what I want you to find out, isn't it?"

"Yeah, okay," Bascomb said, getting to his feet. "I'll find out."

"And do it quick," the Man said. "If the Gunsmith is coming for me, I want to know."

Bascomb wanted to say, if he was coming for you you'd be dead already, but he held his tongue.

"Okay," he said, instead, "I'll get right on it."

"See that you do!"

Once Bascomb was gone, the Man poured himself a drink from his private stock, which he never shared. He never offered anyone a drink when they came to his office. This whiskey was too good for that.

He sipped his drink and tried to calm down. The meeting with Clint Adams had been very civil, until the end, when the man had the nerve to reject him.

He has the feeling that Bascomb would not be able to handle the job if he wanted the Gunsmith killed. He also

CHICAGO CONFIDENTIAL 73

didn't think Slater would be up to it. Maybe the two of them together... except that they'd never be able to work together.

He might have to bring somebody in from outside, but he had time to make up his mind. First, he needed to find out what John Callan had up his sleeve, the old bastard.

"So that was the Gunsmith, huh?" Slater said to Bascomb as they walked to the front door.

"That was him," Bascomb said.

"Didn't seem like so much."

"You don't think so?"

"Well, no... I mean, him sayin' that stuff about his reputation. Me, I'd be braggin' about a rep like that, if I had it."

"Yeah, you would," Bascomb said.

"What's that mean?"

"Just what you said," Bascomb said. "You'd be bragging, if you had anything to brag about."

"Hey—"

Bascomb turned as they reached the door. Slater was reaching out for him, and he dodged the big hand.

"Relax, big guy," Bascomb said. "Your hero can still be your hero. Believe me, he's good."

"He ain't my hero."

"Suit yourself," Bascomb said. "I've got work to do."

Bascomb left and Slater locked the door behind him, muttering, "I ain't got no hero. That's for kids."

Clint started to walk back to the hotel, but as he got to the corner two men appeared, one from either side of him. They had their hands in the pockets of their coats.

"You Adams?" one of them asked.

"That's right."

"Somebody wants ta see you," the other one said.

"Is that a fact?"

"Yeah, it is," the first one said. "There don't have to be no trouble unless you make it."

"Our boss just wants ta talk to ya," the second man said.

"About what?"

"We don't know," the first man said. "We was just sent to get you."

"Get me?"

"Bring ya," the second man said.

"How about ask me?" Clint said. "Invite me."

"Hey, sure," the first man said. "Whatever you wanna call it."

"You guys have guns?" Clint asked.

"Sure, we do," the second man said.

"I've got one, too."

"Like I said," the first man replied, "there don't got to be no trouble unless you want it."

"Yeah, I heard you say that before," Clint said. "Okay, how do we get there?"

One of the men waved and a carriage pulled up. One of the men opened the door for Clint to climb in, and they piled in after him. Then the first man banged on the side of the carriage and they were off.

Outside, Bascomb stopped on the street and looked both ways. He saw Adams on the corner talking to two men, and then a carriage pulled up and the two men pushed Adams into it.

As the carriage pulled away, Bascomb ran to the corner, looking around frantically for a cab.

NINETEEN

They took Clint to a building on East Huron Street, just off of Michigan Avenue. They walked him in and toward the elevator.

"Can we take the stairs?" he asked.

"Whaddaya, afraid of an elevator?" the first man asked. "Fella with a big rep like you?"

"We just don't have any where I'm from," Clint said. "I'm not used to them."

"Safe as can be," the second man said, "unless the cable snaps. Then we fall and die."

Clint did not appreciate the humor. The two men laughed as the elevator started up, stopped at the fourth floor.

"End of the hall," the first man said. The dim light of the hallway gave Clint the chance to look at the men's coats and to see the outline of the guns in their pockets.

The first man knocked when the trio reached the door. It was opened by a woman wearing a gray tweed suit, which failed to hide her opulent curves.

"Miss Tate," the first man said. "We got Clint Adams for Mr. Callan."

"Very well," she said. "I'll take him from here."

"We gotta take his gun," the first man said.

She gave him a disgusted look. "You didn't do that yet? It's a wonder you're not both dead already."

"But we gotta—"

"Never mind," she said. "I don't expect Mr. Adams to be shooting up the place." She looked at Clint. "Please come in, Mr. Adams."

"Thank you."

She closed the door behind him, then walked to a small but expensive-looking secretary's desk. It was very interesting to watch her walk. She looked like she could be a very-well-preserved forty, with lots of honey-colored hair pinned up.

"I hope those two idiots weren't too rough on you," she said.

"I managed."

She smiled and said, "I thought you might. Did they tell you who you were coming to see?"

"Not a clue."

"I work for a man named John Callan. Do you know the name?"

"No."

"Well, we understand you just went to see a competitor of Mr. Callan's."

"Ah, so your boss is another crime boss?"

"Mr. Callan is a businessman," she said, "but some people have referred to him that way."

"So now that I've been to see Rodney Hughes, your boss wants to see me, too?"

She stared at him, obviously impressed.

"I see you've done your research," she said. "You didn't refer to Hughes by name in his presence, did you?"

"I'm afraid I did."

"That couldn't have been pleasant for you," she said.

"Like I said," he answered, "I managed."

"Well, Mr. Callan has left instructions that you be shown in as soon as you arrive. I, uh, don't suppose I could have you give me your gun?"

"I don't think so," he said. "Besides, it's kind of small. Really wouldn't do that much damage to anything but skin and bones."

"I see. Can I get you some coffee or tea? Mr. Callan will offer you some fine brandy, I'm sure."

"Why don't we wait and see what happens?" Clint suggested.

"Very well, then," she said. "Why don't we go in?"

TWENTY

She opened the door to John Callan's office and allowed Clint to enter first. This office was a lot more spartan and businesslike than Rodney Hughes's office had been. The desk was larger, but then the man behind it was also larger, as well as older—probably by thirty years. He had salt-and-pepper hair, which was slicked back and an unlined, pink-skinned face. A cigar stuck out of his mouth. His suit was expensive, but it had to be because it had been tailored to fit his bulk.

"Mr. Adams," he said, rising but remaining behind the desk.

"Mr. Callan."

Clint approached the desk and shook the man's proffered hand. He had a bone-crushing handshake. If this was how strong he was at sixty, Clint was glad he hadn't met the man when he was thirty.

"Please, have a seat," Callan said. "Can I pour you some wonderful brandy?"

"You can."

"Excellent."

A sidebar was kept very close to his desk so that he didn't have to move very much to get to it. He poured two glasses and pushed one across to Clint.

"Thank you."

"I understand you just came from seeing one of my competitors," Callan said.

"Rodney Hughes?"

"Yes," Callan said with a laugh. "He calls himself 'the Man.'"

"Yes, he does. But . . . one of your competitors? How many crime bosses does Chicago have?"

"I really don't like that name, but if you were to ask me, there's only one: myself. The newspapers would tell you otherwise."

"So would Rodney be your biggest competitor?"

"I'm afraid so," he said. "I hate the little punk. He's got no respect."

"He is kind of young," Clint conceded.

"He aligned himself with the right people when he got to town," Callan said. "Became the number one to a good friend of mine, but quickly killed him and took over his action. And he's got a good number one, himself."

"Bascomb?"

Callan nodded. "Good man," he said.

"What about Slater?"

"He's just muscle," Callan said, dismissing the man. "A bodyguard. Of no consequence."

"And you have Miss Tate?"

Callan smiled. "She's my secretary, and I couldn't operate without her."

"I can understand that," Clint said, sipping his drink. "I wonder, Mr. Callan, if we could get to why I've been brought here."

For the first time, Callan took the cigar from his mouth, but just long enough to sip his drink, then the cigar went right back in.

"To the point. I like that. I know your reputation," Callan said. "I also know that reputations tend to be bloated."

"I agree with you there."

"I thought you might," Callan said. "Do you mind if I ask what you and Hughes talked about?"

"Well," Clint said, "maybe we should talk about what you want, first."

"Very well," Callan said. "First, I don't want you to work with Hughes. Next, I don't wan't you to work for any of my other competitors. And finally, I want you to do some work for me."

"What kind of work did you have in mind?" Clint asked.

"Well, what kind of work do you normally do?" Callan asked.

"Well, I fix guns," Clint said.

"But the Gunsmith name . . ."

"It's not just a name," Clint said.

"That's your profession?"

"That part of my reputation is right."

"Well, I don't need that part of your expertise," Callan said. "What I'm interested in is more what you can do with a gun in your hand."

"So, even though you understand that reputations are bloated, you want me to kill for you."

"Well, I know what newspapermen and dime-novel writers do with the facts," Callan said, "but I also know there's a germ of truth in everything. You have killed men with your gun, haven't you?"

"Yes, but as I told the Man," Clint answered, "never anyone who wasn't threatening me, or trying to kill me first."

"In Chicago," John Callan said, "everybody's trying to kill you."

"Not me," Clint said. "I don't live here."

"Well," Callan said, "I have people trying to kill me, and I'd like to kill them first."

"Go ahead."

"I want you to do it."

"Why?"

"Because then I can safely say none of my people did it."

"You know," Clint said, "it seems to me that since you and the Man are both crime bosses, you have plenty of men to do your killing. Also seems to me you probably have plenty of money to bring somebody in."

"I do," Callan said. "I want to bring you in."

"I'm not for hire."

"Don't you want to know how much I would pay you?" Callan asked.

"I'm not for sale, and neither is my gun."

Callan firmed his jaw and sat back in his chair. The leather groaned.

"I don't take being told no lightly, Mr. Adams."

"Well," Clint said, "then you and Rodney have a lot in common." He put the half-empty glass back on the desk. "Thanks for the drink."

He stood up, headed for the door, then stopped and turned back.

"If either of your men try to stop me, I'll consider myself threatened."

TWENTY-ONE

"Finished already?" Miss Tate asked. "I thought there would be some lengthy negotiating."

"It doesn't take much negotiating to say no, Miss Tate," Clint said.

She put her hands over her mouth. "You said no to him?"

"It was the only answer that made any sense."

"But . . . nobody ever says no to him," she said. "Now I have to work with him the rest of the day."

"Well, I can solve that," he said. "Let's go out and have some lunch. Or supper?"

"W-what?" she said. "You're asking me to lunch?"

"Well, since I just made your boss mad I figured it's the least I can do. Then that way we can get to know one another better."

"Well . . . I don't know . . ." she said. "I'd have to check—"

"Why don't we just surprise him and leave?" Clint suggested.

"Oh, I couldn't do that," she said, "much as I might like to. He's my boss."

"Sounds like he's a lot of people's boss," Clint said. "But he's not going to be mine."

Clint headed for the door, but stopped when he got there.

"Are those two going to be out there when I go out?" he asked.

"Out where?"

"In the hall."

"Shouldn't be," she said. "Their job was just to . . . escort you here."

"Maybe we could have that lunch another time?"

"Well . . . yes, I'd like that."

"Good," he said. "I'll call on you another time."

"Yes, all right. I'll look forward to it."

Clint nodded, then opened the door. The hallway was empty. He found the stairway and walked down the four flights, expecting to find the two men in the lobby. He was happy to find they weren't there; he didn't feel like shooting anybody. That certainly wasn't what he had come to Chicago for.

He stepped outside, found the street empty, turned, and walked to a corner to find a cab.

After Clint left, Miss Tate went into John Callan's office.

"Sit down."

She did.

"Does he like you?" he asked.

"Yes, he asked me to go to lunch."

"Why didn't you go?"

"He wanted me to just walk out without telling you. I couldn't do that."

CHICAGO CONFIDENTIAL 89

"You should have," Callan said.

"I wanted him to know that you're my boss and I'm loyal to you."

"Okay, fine. How did you leave it?"

"That we'd have lunch another time."

"When?"

"He said he'd call on me."

"That's not good enough," Callan said. "We'll have to arrange something."

"Like what?"

"I'll let you know," he said.

She sat there, waiting.

"That's all, Miss Tate."

"Yes, sir."

She left his office and sat at her own desk.

Bascomb watched as Clint Adams came out of the building, walked to the corner, and managed to wave down a cab. When he was gone he crossed the street and entered the building. Bascomb was sure that no one had seen him go in, but he took the stairs so he wouldn't run into anyone coming down in the elevator.

When he got to the fourth floor, he stuck his head into the hall to make sure it was empty. This was more of a chance than he liked to take, but he needed the advantage the situation presented.

He padded down the hall quickly, tried to turn the door knob, and found the door unlocked. He opened the door and peered in. Miss Tate was at her desk, and she was alone.

"Psst," he said, sticking his head in.

She looked up from her desk and her eyes widened.

"What are you doing here?" she demanded in a whisper.

"We need to talk."

"Not now! Not here."

"When?"

"Give me an hour."

"Where?"

"Meet me at J.T.'s," she told him.

"Okay, one hour."

"Yes! Now go! Before somebody sees you."

He nodded, withdrew his head, and closed the door. He managed to get back down the hall and the stairs to the lobby without being seen.

TWENTY-TWO

Bascomb was sitting at a table in J.T.'s, what he called a hole in the wall. Since it was only two blocks from Callan's office, he had always wondered why none of Callan's people went in there. So far, it had been a safe place for him and Nina to meet—there and the room upstairs.

Nina Tate walked in, looking harried. She looked around quickly, saw Bascomb and walked over. He had nabbed a corner table, so her face would be hidden from anyone who walked in.

"I got you a glass of brandy," he said, nodding at the glass on the table.

"Thank you."

"Do you want to have some supper?"

"Yes," she said, "I'm hungry."

She had been hungry when Clint Adams invited her to eat, but she couldn't go yet. Now she was famished, but she was also nervous to be seen so close to the office with Bascomb.

"Maybe we should go someplace else?" she asked.

"No, this is fine," he said. "You're sure nobody from Callan's crew comes here?"

"No," she said, "they prefer a saloon somewhere."

"Okay, then," he said. "Let's eat."

"I don't want to eat," she said. "Let's go upstairs instead."

Bascomb had cultivated Nina Tate months earlier, when the Man told him he wanted him to have contacts inside Callan's business. He let the Man think that he had several contacts, when in fact he had just one: Callan's personal secretary.

Nina believed he was interested in her as a man is interested in a woman. Bascomb had checked her out first, and thought she'd be too smart to fall for his act but, in fact, she wasn't. She'd reacted to it just like he thought a woman would.

To get to the room upstairs, they had to come outside and go in a second door next to the first one. Once inside, they came together, undoing buttons and fasteners until all their clothes were off. Nina was usually eager, but today she seemed driven by desperation.

He cupped her large breasts in his hands, kissed and licked the nipples until they were hard. She moved her hands over him, squeezing his buttocks, stroking his thighs, reaching between and grabbing hold of his hard cock.

"Come on, come on," she implored, tugging him toward the bed. They fell on it together, their hot flesh pressing together. She rolled him over so she could straddle him and then took her hair down, shaking it out before she sat down hard on him, taking him inside. She gasped and shuddered and then started riding him up and down. He watched her, as in her desperation she seemed oblivious to the fact that he was there, except for his cock. Her eyes were closed and she bit her lip each time she came down on him, harder and harder. He began to lift his hips to meet her each time she came down, and she grunted when they came together. Then, suddenly, the cords on her neck stood out, her body trembled, and she fell onto him as the tremors coursed through her body. She clung to him, her nails digging in, and when he exploded inside of her she cried out and scratched him . . .

"Clint Adams came to our office, right from your boss's," she told him later, as they lay together, she in the crook of his arm.

"Is that a fact?"

"He turned Callan down," she said. "Can you imagine?"

"Told my boss the same thing," Bascomb said.

"Then he's as good as dead, isn't he?" she asked. "Telling them both no? One of them is going to have him killed."

"I suppose so."

"Would he have you do it?" she asked.

"I don't know," he said. "Maybe."

"And if he did, would you?"

"Maybe we better get going," he said . . .

As they dressed, Bascomb was careful not to ask any questions about her boss. It was the way he always tried to work it, so that it was she who brought up her boss, not him.

"If your boss doesn't send you after Adams, who would he send? Slater?"

"Adams would eat Slater up."

"Then who?"

"I don't know," he said. "Somebody from outside the organization, I suppose."

"Is he as famous as they say?"

"He's as famous," Bascomb said, "but there's no telling if he's as good as they say. Somebody would have to find that out."

She reached out and touched his hand. "Not you."

"Maybe."

"Promise me you'll be careful?" she asked.

"I'm always careful, Nina."

She rubbed his hand, then withdrew hers.

When they left the building, he went out, looked both ways to make sure the street was clear, and then let her come out.

"In the future, we'll meet somewhere else," he said.

"And you won't come to the office," she said, touching his face. "It's too dangerous for you."

"And for you," he said. "No, I won't do that again."

"When can we be together again?" she asked.

"Soon," he said, "very soon. I promise."

"All right."

She squeezed his hand, then turned and walked away. He waited until she was out of sight, then turned and went the other way.

Clint had stopped the cab just around the corner and said, "I'm getting out."

"What? You just got in."

He paid the cabbie and walked back to the corner, peered around just in time to see Bascomb cross over and go in. He'd spotted him in the doorway across the street, and wanted him to think he'd left and gone back to the hotel.

He waited outside until Bascomb came out again, then followed him, turning the tables on the man. Bascomb only went two blocks and stepped into a restaurant called J.T.'s.

Clint peered in the window and watched the man order a drink but nothing to eat. Instinctively, he felt Bascomb was waiting for someone. He decided to go across the street, find a doorway of his own, and wait.

It was almost an hour before Nina Tate arrived. She looked around nervously before stepping into the restaurant. Once again, Clint peered in a window, and saw the two of them sitting together. In a few minutes, they came out and went through another door. Probably to a room upstairs.

He settled into his doorway for a long wait.

It wasn't actually that long before they came out. He witnessed the scene from when they came out. The way she touched his face, it was obvious she had feelings for Bascomb, but whether Bascomb felt the same or was just using her remained to be seen.

When they had both left, Clint stepped from the doorway. He walked a few blocks before he could wave down a passing cab, and finally headed back to his hotel with more information than he'd bargained for.

TWENTY-THREE

Back at his hotel, he gave in to his own hunger and went into the hotel dining room. He lingered over a meal, enjoying the food, and replaying the day's events in his head. After leaving the office of John Callan, he had wondered if he'd made a bad enemy. Now he had to wonder if he'd made two. Leaving Chicago was starting to look like a much more viable solution. He didn't have any reason to want to bring either man down. They were probably going to do that to each other, eventually. Staying in town would only be the stubborn thing to do, not wanting to be driven out. But that would be giving in to his ego, something he usually felt he was in control of.

He finished eating, crossed the lobby, and entered the Bull & Calf. It was the last day of the week and the place was packed, with a mixture of guests and local businessmen.

He approached the bar and caught the eye of Seamus.

"Beer?" the Irishman asked.

"You bet."

"Comin' up."

When Seamus brought the beer he said, "There's been a fella here waitin' about an hour for you."

"Where?"

"Over your left shoulder, sittin' alone, nursing a beer."

"Do you know anything about him?" Clint asked.

"I know a lot about him," Seamus said.

"What's the most important thing you know?" Clint asked.

"Well, that would either be that he's a countryman of mine," Seamus said, "or that he's a policeman."

"A policeman!"

"One of Chicago's finest," Seamus said. "A young lieutenant of detectives. What kind of trouble have you been getting yerself into?"

"None, yet," Clint said. "Did you tell him you'd point me out to him?"

"I did say that, aye," Seamus said, losing control of his accent, "but I never intended to."

"That's okay," Clint said. "I'll go and announce myself. In fact, give me a fresh beer for the lieutenant."

Armed with both beers, he walked over to the man's table and set them down.

"I understand you've been waiting for me," he said.

The man looked up at him with the eyes of a child. Clint had to wonder right from the start if this was an act.

"And you are?" the young man asked.

"Clint Adams."

"Oh, yes, Mr. Adams," the man said. "Indeed, I have been asking about you. That barman was supposed to point you out when you came in."

"I told him not to bother," Clint said. "Here you go, a fresh beer."

"Well . . ."

"It's okay," Clint said. "I'm not trying to bribe you."

"No, of course not," the man said. "Well, thanks. Have a seat, please."

Clint sat, stared at the young man. He was about Rodney Hughes's age.

"What can I do for you . . . Lieutenant, is it?" Clint asked.

"I'm sorry," the policeman said, "I haven't introduced myself. I'm Lieutenant Patrick Muldoon, Chicago Police Department."

"I understand you're a lieutenant of detectives. That's an impressive title for someone so young."

"I'm not as young as I look, I'm afraid," Muldoon said. "I'm thirty-four."

"Still young, by my standards."

Clint sipped his beer and waited for the lieutenant to get to the point, even though he thought he knew what the point was.

"Mr. Adams, you haven't been in Chicago very long, and yet you've already been known to visit with some of our more infamous citizens."

"Infamous?"

"Undesirable, one might even say."

"Like who?"

"Well, for one, Robert Pinkerton."

"I didn't know Pinkertons were undesirables."

"Well, to a lot of policemen, they are," Muldoon said. "Also, a man named Rodney Hughes who goes by the name 'the Man.'" Muldoon rolled his eyes to let Clint know what he thought of the affectation.

"Is that all?"

"For starters," Muldoon said. Clint had the feeling his visit to Callan had been too recent to be discovered. And yet, how had any of the visits come to the attention of the police?

"Mr. Adams," Muldoon said, "I'm afraid I have to ask you what your purpose was for coming to Chicago."

"I'm going to tell you the same thing I told Pinkerton and Hughes," Clint said. "I came for a rest."

"A rest?" Muldoon asked. "You'll forgive me, but a man like you isn't particularly known for taking rests."

Although Muldoon was a countryman of Seamus's, there was no hint of an accent. Clint wondered if, like the bartender, this was by design.

"That may be," Clint said, "but men like me tend to need a lot more rest than most people."

"That's probably true," Muldoon said. "I stand corrected. But you should know, if you do not know already, that there is a war going on in Chicago, and warriors from out of town have been brought in from time to time."

"I see," Clint said. "So you think I'm an imported warrior?"

"It's something we've considered," Muldoon said. "I just thought I'd come and see you and ask you straight out."

"Okay, then," Clint said. "Ask your question, and I'll answer it."

"Very well." The young lieutenant cleared his throat, then took a sip of beer. "Are you in Chicago to sell your gun?"

TWENTY-FOUR

"And, of course, by sell your gun I don't mean your actual gun, I mean—"

"I know what the question means, Lieutenant," Clint said, cutting him off.

Muldoon looked momentarily . . . shocked? Offended? "Sorry," he said.

"Let me make this as clear as I can," Clint said. "I told the same thing to Rodney Hughes. I do not sell my gun to anyone, not even the highest bidder. I came to Chicago to get away from people who want to buy my gun."

"I see."

"Do you?" Clint asked. "Do you really? Because nobody else seems to."

"Nobody?" Muldoon asked. "By that you mean . . . Hughes? And . . . anyone else?"

Clint decided to tell the truth, in case Muldoon had good contacts and would find out, anyway.

"I just came from a meeting with a man named John Callan."

Muldoon sat back and stared at him.

"For someone new in town, you certainly are getting around," the policeman said.

"I didn't ask to see Hughes or Callan," Clint said truthfully, "and I went to Robert Pinkerton just to get some information because I never heard of either man."

"Are you friends with Mr. Pinkerton?"

"Just acquaintances," Clint said. "I knew his father."

Muldoon raised his eyebrows and said, "That's impressive."

"I knew him," Clint said, "I didn't say I liked him."

"You're either being very truthful with me, or you want me to believe you are being very truthful," Muldoon said.

"Well, I guess that's something you're going to have to decide for yourself, Lieutenant."

"So where do you stand with Mr. Hughes and Mr. Callan?"

"I don't think either of them likes me very much," Clint said. "Given their reputations in this town, I suppose that's not very healthy for me."

"Are you going to leave Chicago?"

"I haven't made up my mind yet."

"You know we can't have any shoot-outs on Michigan Avenue," the policeman said.

"I don't intend to get into any public shoot-outs, Lieutenant," Clint said. "Of course, the final decision may not be mine."

"You're thinking they may come after you?" Muldoon asked.

"Apparently, neither of them likes to be told no," Clint said.

"Perhaps leaving town would be the best course of action for you."

Clint's ego bristled. Now he was being run out of town by the law as well as the crime bosses?

"I've got a question for you," Clint said.

"What is it?"

"How many more crime bosses can I expect to try to recruit me?"

"Well, there are others, but you've already seen the two major forces in Chicago crime," Muldoon said. "I don't think you'll hear from the others."

"That's good."

"Unless . . ."

"Unless what?"

"Unless they try to kill you to keep you from working for the top two."

"Thanks," Clint said, "that's very reassuring."

TWENTY-FIVE

Clint walked with Lieutenant Muldoon as far as the bar, then watched as the policeman walked out the door to the street.

"Everythin' okay?" Seamus asked.

"No problems," Clint said. Unless you considered Chicago's top crime boss's planning your demise a problem.

He stared at Seamus for a few seconds while the man served another patron a beer. Somebody in the hotel was working for either the Man or the police. Hell, Callan may even have had someone in there. He wondered which side of the law the big Irishman was on, if any?

As Seamus came back over to him, Clint pushed his partially finished beer over to him and said, "Freshen that up, will you?"

"Sure thing."

When he returned, Seamus asked, "The police givin' ya a hard time?"

"Not so much. I'm kind of used to dealing with the law."

"Yeah, I got that impression from you."

"What impression was that?"

"That you're a man who can handle 'imself."

Clint tried to remember if he'd told Seamus his name, full or otherwise. The desk clerk certainly knew it—or any desk clerk, for that matter. It didn't have to be the one who'd checked him in. Also, any bellhop who got a look at the register could have sold the information.

He stood there for about fifteen minutes before Seamus returned and eyed his half-full mug.

"Nursin' that one?"

"I'm going to turn in," Clint said. "Nobody else has been looking for me, have they?"

"Not in here," Seamus said. "You might wanna check at the desk."

"Yeah, I'm kind of thinking that somebody with access to the desk might be selling information around town."

"To who?"

Clint shrugged.

"The police, or somebody on the other side of the law."

"You mean like sellin' your name from the register?" the big Irishman asked.

"That's what I'm thinking."

"Is your name worth that much?" Seamus asked.

"Somebody might think so."

Seamus leaned on the bar.

"Don't suppose you wanna clue me in to the secret, do ya, now?"

"Clint Adams," Clint said. "My name is Clint Adams."

Seamus stood up.

"I know that name," he said. "You're some kinda legend in the West, right?"

"I don't feel much like a legend, but yeah, I guess you could say that."

"Well, sure," Seamus said, "the clerk and bellhops in this place ain't above sellin' some information."

"That's what I thought."

"And were you thinkin' the same might be true of me?" the big man asked.

"The thought crossed my mind."

"Well, I didn't know your name before," Seamus said, "and now that I do, it seems like anybody who's anybody probably has it already. Am I right?"

"I think so."

The bartender shrugged his big shoulders. "Don't much matter to me, then," he said. "I do kinda wonder what you're doin' in Chicago, but I also guess you just went through that with the police."

"You'd be guessing right."

"Well," Seamus said, standing up straight, "if anybody else comes in lookin' for ya, I'll be sure to let ya know."

"I'd appreciate it."

"Hey," Seamus said, "it's the least I can do for a visitin' legend."

"This legend is saying good-night."

Seamus laughed and turned to serve his other customers.

Clint left the bar and crossed the lobby, looking for anyone who might be paying him special attention—or someone who was trying to look like they weren't paying him any attention. As he passed the desk, he exchanged nods with the clerk who'd checked him in. He could have approached the young man, but he decided to keep him as a secret weapon, just in case the man wanted to pass on some false information along the way.

For now he was really just thinking about the soft bed in his room.

TWENTY-SIX

After her meeting with Carter Bascomb, Nina Tate had gone back to her office to take care of some paperwork before she finally went home. She did not expect to find John Callan there, but he was. He came to his office door and stared at her from behind his ever-present cigar.

"Where'd you go?" he demanded. Gone was the polished speech he had used on Clint Adams. Callan was a thug who'd grown up on the streets of Chicago, and most of the time he talked and acted like one.

"I went to dinner."

"Whaddaya doin' back here?"

"I have some paperwork I wanted to finish."

"Forget about it," he said. "I got a job for you."

"What is it?"

"I want you to find out what you can from Clint Adams."

"How am I supposed to do that?" she asked. "He did say he would call for lunch. I could—"

"Forget that!" he said. He took the cigar out of his mouth. The end of it was a wet mess, and she averted her eyes.

"I want you to go to his hotel tonight," he said. "Go to his room. Do what you have to do to get him to talk. You understand?"

She understood. She owed Callan a lot for getting her off the streets and giving her a job. All she had to do was keep his office running, and do these extra jobs for him on occasion. It had been a while since he'd asked her, though. She had thought that maybe they were past that. Obviously, that wasn't the case.

"Go home and put somethin' on," he said. "You know the kinda thing I like."

"Yes, I do."

"And don't look like that when you see him."

"Like what?"

"Like you're walkin' to the hangman," he said. "It's just sex, an' you done that before, ain't ya?"

"Yes," she said, "I have."

"An' it's been a while," he said, leering, "but if I remember right, you really like it."

She nodded and started for the door.

"We got a desk clerk there on the payroll," he said. "You know the one. He'll let you into Adams's room. Unless you'd rather knock, like a lady."

She went out the door, and just barely kept herself from slamming it.

And that was why, as Clint Adams made his way to his room, Nina Tate was in his room, in his bed, waiting for him. She pondered doing that naked, but considered what her boss had said about her being a lady, and kept her nightgown on.

She hoped against hope that she'd be able to keep this little adventure from Carter Bascomb. If he found out that she did these kinds of jobs for John Callan, it would surely ruin what they had together.

And if she had any courage at all, she would quit her job with Callan. But in truth she had still not worked off her debt to him. He'd taken her off the streets, made her his mistress for a short time, and then his private secretary, with a very good paycheck. But it wasn't the money that tied her to him, it was the gratitude. Only he threw it in her face so often that she was starting to run out.

Maybe this would finally be the last time she did a job like this for him.

Maybe after this, the debt would be paid.

TWENTY-SEVEN

As Clint approached his room, he saw the light shining from beneath the door. He had not left the lamp on. He took the gun from his belt, held it in his left hand, and opened the door with his right.

"I thought a man like you would have a suite," Nina Tate said from his bed. "Not that I'm not impressed that you're even staying at the Templar. This room is still quite nice."

He entered and looked around before closing the door behind him. Considering who she worked for, he wanted to be sure she hadn't brought some help with her.

"Miss Tate," he said, closing the door behind him. "What are you doing here?"

"Well, you said you'd call on me for lunch," she said, "but I really couldn't wait."

"And why is that?"

"Because you're a fascinating man," she said. "Not like anyone else I know in Chicago. After all, you are—"

"Don't say a legend of the West, please," Clint said. "I've heard that enough for one day."

"And you're modest," she said. "See what I mean? You're very different."

Her curvaceous body was clad in a diaphanous nightgown rather than a buttoned-down tweed suit. Her big breasts were on display, as was her pale skin. The honey-colored hair that had been atop her head was now cascading down over her shoulders and breasts, dark nipples peeking out from behind it. The lower half of her body was underneath the bed sheet.

Clint put his gun down on a nearby dresser, but didn't move far from it. He still wasn't sure she hadn't been sent there to distract him while a couple of killers came bursting through the door.

"Why are you standing all the way over there?" she asked, playing with her hair.

"I'm not yet sure what you're doing here," he answered. "Or what I'm going to do."

"I know what we're going to do," she told him.

"Were you sent here to seduce me, Miss Tate," he said, "or distract me?"

"Distract you?"

"While a couple of killers get into position," he said.

She picked up the bed sheet and peered underneath.

"No killers here," she said coyly. "Wanna come look?"

Clint walked to the bed, accepting the fact that he and Miss Tate were alone. Now he wanted to find out why.

He sat next to her on the bed. Everything about her was softer than the last time he'd seen her. She was very beautiful.

"What's your first name?" he asked.

"Nina. And you're Clint?"

"That's right. Nina. What are you doing here?"

"I told you—"

"You're a beautiful woman," he said. "And intelligent, if I'm any judge."

"Why . . . thank you." She looked suddenly shy.

"Which leads me back to my question: Why are you here? You have no reason to sneak into a man's room, or his bed. I think you could have any man you choose."

"And you don't believe I've chosen you?"

"No," he said, "I don't."

She removed the shoulder straps of her gown to reveal her full breasts. They were rounded and full, pale and smooth, topped with dark brown nipples that were not distended. He'd been with enough women to know when they were sexually excited, and she was not.

Clint reached for her gown and pulled it back up to cover her.

"I assume you have clothes that you brought with you?" he asked.

"Yes." She put her arms across her breasts, hands on her shoulders, as if she was suddenly cold—or ashamed.

"Then put them on," he said. "Then we'll talk. I'll wait in the hall. Let me know when you're finished."

He stepped out into the hall until she opened the door, fully clothed. She was wearing a dress that buttoned to the neck, and had put her hair up. Her appearance was something between what he'd seen in the office, and what he'd seen in his bed.

He came back in and closed the door. She turned her back to him, as if still ashamed.

"Your boss sent you here, didn't he?"

She nodded.

"You don't have any need to be ashamed," he said.

"Don't I?"

"No."

He walked to her and touched her shoulders. She flinched for a moment, but did not pull away.

"If I thought you were here because you wanted to be, I would've jumped into bed with you in a minute."

"I . . . appreciate that."

He dropped his hands.

"He wanted you to pump me for information, right?"

"Yes," she said. "To find out all I could."

"There's no more I can tell you that I didn't tell your boss," he said. "I came here for my own reasons, none that have anything to do with your boss's business. Or anyone else's. I have no connections in Chicago."

She turned to face him. "If I tell him that, he won't believe me."

"He'll believe that it's what I told you," he said. "You can tell him that you believed me, or not."

"If I tell him I didn't believe you, he'll have you killed."

"Maybe," Clint said, "but I think that either he or the Man are going to try that, anyway."

"Then you should leave Chicago."

"That's one solution."

"And another solution would be for you to kill them before they can kill you?" she asked.

"No," he said. "I don't like that as an alternative. I'll defend myself, but I won't go after them." He looked at her. "Try telling him that."

"You want me to tell him . . . the truth?"

"Yes," Clint said. "And tell him you got it . . . well, any way you want him to believe. If you want to tell him you seduced it out of me, that's fine."

"Why are you being so nice to me?" she asked. "I was prepared to seduce information out of you."

"Prepared," he said, "but not willingly. Isn't that so?"

"Well, yes . . ."

"That suits me, Nina," Clint said. "You tell your boss anything he needs to know to keep yourself safe."

She stared at him, then went to him and kissed him on the cheek.

"I wish I had come on my own, Clint," she said.

He smiled at her.

"Anytime you want to come back on your own," he said, "just let me know."

She smiled back and said, "I'll do that."

She picked up her jacket, then turned to face him.

"Be very careful, Clint Adams," she said. "John Callan isn't the man you met. And I'd be willing to bet the same is true of your other meeting."

"Thank you, Nina," he said. "I'll keep that in mind."

TWENTY-EIGHT

Sleep came grudgingly. Nina had left her heady scent on his sheets. When he did fall asleep, he dreamed that she had dropped her nightgown, only this time he didn't pull it back up. He awoke painfully erect, and did his best to ignore the condition.

He washed, wishing he had colder water, and went down to breakfast. He asked the waiter to bring him the thickest steak he had, with eggs and strong coffee, hoping that would distract him.

He was just starting on his breakfast when Carter Bascomb walked into the dining room, looked around, and then approached him.

"Buy me breakfast," he said.

"Sure, have a seat."

Clint told the waiter to bring Bascomb the same thing.

"What can I do for you this morning," Clint asked, "besides buy you breakfast?"

"Tell me about your meeting with John Callan."

"You know all about my meeting with Callan."

Bascomb poured himself a cup of coffee from the pot on the table.

"Because his personal secretary, Nina Tate, is your girlfriend."

Bascomb stopped with the cup halfway to his mouth.

"What makes you say that?" he asked.

"You're not the only one who is good at following people," Clint said. "I saw you meet her at J.T.'s. And I saw the two of you outside. I can read the signs."

"You got into a cab," Bascomb said. "I saw you ride away."

"And stop around the corner," Clint said. "I knew you were watching me."

Bascomb sipped his coffee, then set the cup down.

"Maybe I'm getting old."

"No," Clint said, "maybe you just have to admit that somebody else might be as good as you are."

"Or better?"

"I didn't say that."

Bascomb drank more coffee.

"If your boss wants me killed, will he send you after me?"

"Probably."

"And will you kill me?"

"I'll do my job," Bascomb said, "but I won't be happy about it."

"Why not?"

The waiter arrived with Bascomb's breakfast. He sat back to allow the meal to be set in front of him and said, "Who else would buy me meals like this?"

"Tell me about Nina," Clint said a little later.

"What about her?"

"She is your girlfriend, right?" Clint asked.

"I needed somebody inside Callan's organization," Bascomb said.

"She's in love with you."

"That was the point," Bascomb said, "to get her to fall in love with me so I could get information."

"And that's all she means to you?"

"That's it," Bascomb said with a shrug.

"She came to my room last night," Clint said, watching Bascomb's face.

"Is that a fact?"

Clint nodded. "She was in my bed when I got there."

"Good for you, I guess," Bascomb said. "She does that kind of thing for Callan."

"That's what I figured."

"So you didn't sleep with her?"

"Would you care if I did?"

"No."

Clint believed him, and felt sorry for poor Nina.

"Well, I sent her back to Callan with the truth," Clint said. "I don't know what he'll do with it."

"Probably try to kill you," Bascomb said.

"Probably," Clint said. "I guess I'll have to wait and see who comes first, you or him. Meanwhile, I've been contacted by someone from the other side."

"The other side?"

"Lieutenant Muldoon of the Chicago Police Department."

"That idiot?" Bascomb said. "He's a kid trying to make a name for himself."

"Kid? He's about your boss's age."

"Actually," Bascomb said, "he's older, but that doesn't matter. He's too damn naïve to be any kind of danger."

"You sure it's not an act?" Clint asked.

"I'm positive."

"Well, maybe—"

"You think I could enjoy the rest of this meal?" Bascomb asked. "Just in case it's my last one, for a while?"

"By all means," Clint said, "Enjoy."

TWENTY-NINE

When Nina Tate got to work that morning, John Callan was waiting.

"So?" he asked. "Did you succeed?"

"Yes, I did."

"Good," the man said. "Come into my office and tell me what you found out."

She followed him in.

Fifteen minutes later, she finished talking. He puffed furiously on his cigar.

"So, he says he's not with anybody."

"Yes."

"And you believed him?"

"Yes."

"If it's true," Callan said, "then he's even more dangerous."

"How do you figure?"

"He could end up working for the law against me," Callan said.

"So what will you do?"

"I'll have to get rid of him," Callan said.

"Kill him?"

"That's what get rid of means, yes," he said.

"But . . . do you even have anyone who could do it?" she asked. "After all, he's the Gunsmith."

"I'll have to bring in somebody very special," Callan said. "I'll show him a Chicago killer can handle anything the West wants to send us—including him."

"But . . ."

"But what?"

"The best man in Chicago for the job works for . . . well, you know."

"Are you talkin' about your boyfriend?"

"My . . . boyfriend?"

"Bascomb."

She stared at him.

He took the cigar from his mouth and used it to point at her. "Do you think I'm stupid, Nina?" he demanded. "I've known about you and Bascomb from the beginning."

"B-but . . . how?"

"There's something about your boyfriend even you don't know," Callan said.

"What's that?"

"You'll find out later," he said. "Now get out and do your job.

"What? Still?"

"Oh yeah," he said. "You're still mine, Nina. That ain't changed."

"I-I don't—"

"Don't say a word," he said. "Go back to your desk and find Jedcoe. I want him here right away. Understand?"

"I understand."

"He'll be able to get me somebody," Callan said. "He knows all the talent. Get me Jedcoe."

"Yes, sir."

On stiff legs, she walked out of the office back to her own desk, and sat down. She didn't know what else to do.

Clint and Bascomb walked out of the dining room together and into the lobby.

"What's on your agenda for today?" Clint asked.

"I don't know," Bascomb said. He sounded disgusted. "I'm getting kind of sick of the whole thing. Whether Callan or Hughes comes out on top, things in Chicago are gonna be just as bad."

"You're saying you don't care who wins this war?"

"Maybe I'm saying," Bascomb replied, "that I don't want either one of them to win."

"Maybe you should talk to the police, then."

"No," Bascomb said, "I can't go that far."

"You'll have to make up your mind at some point."

"Now that," Bascomb said, "is something we agree on."

THIRTY

As Bascomb left the hotel, Clint walked over to the desk. The same clerk who had checked him in was there. He had also been the clerk on duty the night before.

"Mr. Adams," he started, pleasantly, "what can I do—"

Clint cut him off by grabbing the front of his shirt and pulling him across the desk.

"Next time you sell any information about me, or let somebody into my room, I won't take it so easy on you. Understand?"

He pulled the young man completely across the desk and deposited him on the floor.

"Do you understand?" he asked again.

"Y-yessir."

"Now, who do you work for?"

"Um—um—he'll kill me—"

"He's not here," Clint said, "and I am."

"I-I . . . kinda take some money from somebody who works for Mr. Callan. It's just some . . . extra money. I don't mean no harm."

"You don't take money from anybody else?"

"Well—"

A crowd was forming as Clint put his foot on the boy's chest and pushed him flat down onto the floor.

"Come on!"

"I-I take money from guests sometimes, to get them things," he said. "H-hey, all the clerks do it."

"All the clerks take money from gangsters?"

"Well, no, but . . . some of the bellhops—"

"What's going on here?" a man shouted.

Clint turned his head and saw a well-dressed man approaching with a frown on his face. He guessed it was the hotel manager. He decided to make a friend of the clerk, so he reached down and took his hand, yanked him to his feet.

"What's the meaning of this?" the man asked.

"Are you the hotel manager?" Clint asked.

"That's right. My name is Mr. Powell."

"Well, Mr. Powell, your clerk here had some kind of attack. He fell down and I was helping him up."

"Attack?" Powell asked.

"Yes," Clint said, "I think the boy might need to see a doctor."

"Richard? Are you all right?" the manager asked.

"I-I'm okay, Mr. Powell. I-I didn't eat today, that's all. I kinda . . . fainted."

"Richard, you represent this hotel," Powell said. "You have to make sure you're in shape to come to work in the morning. Make sure you have something to eat."

"Yes, sir."

"I'll find someone to cover for you. I want you to go into the dining room and have breakfast right now."

"There'll be no charge for that, right?" Clint asked.

"Huh? Wha— No charge? I, uh—"

Clint slapped Richard on the back and said, "Just put it on my bill, Richard. I'll buy your breakfast."

"Th-thank you, Mr. Adams," Richard said. "I appreciate it."

"Sure."

"Uh, thank you, sir, for your concern," Powell said to Clint.

"Think nothing of it, Mr. Powell," Clint said. "You have a very nice hotel, here. Very nice. Good employees."

"Thank you, sir," Powell said. "We have a lot of pride here at the Templar."

"As you should," Clint said.

He turned and walked away from the desk as Powell and Richard continued to talk, and the crowd began to disperse. He went up the stairs to his room and waited.

About an hour later, there was a knock at his door. He left his gun in his belt, but put his right hand on it as he opened the door with his left.

"Mr. Adams?" Richard, the clerk, said. "Can I come in?"

"Sure, Richard. Come on in."

Clint backed away to let him enter. The young man closed the door and turned to face Clint.

"You coulda got me fired, and you didn't."

"That's not what I'm after, Richard," Clint said. "I don't want you to lose your job."

"I-I . . . if Mr. Powell found out that I was taking money from Mr. Callan's man, that's what would happen."

"I'm not going to tell him," Clint said, "are you?"

"N-no, I'm not," Richard said. "B-but I should tell you—I let that woman into your room last night. I did that for Mr. Callan."

"And when I checked in, did you recognize my name and sell it to Mr. Callan's people?"

"Y-yes, I did that."

"And what about Mr. Hughes? Do you sell information to him?"

"Mr. Hughes?"

"In Chicago they call him 'the Man.'"

Richard's eyes widened and he said, "N-no, I don't have anything to do with him."

"Okay. Do you know of anyone else who works here who does?"

"No, I don't," he said. "I know some of the bellhops take money, you know, to get things for guests, but that's all."

"Okay," Clint said. "You better get back to work before you do lose your job."

"Yes, sir."

As Richard opened the door, Clint asked, "Did you enjoy the breakfast?"

"Oh, yes, sir!" he said. "I've never eaten in the dining room before. Thank you."

"You're welcome."

Richard ducked his head, opened the door, and went out into the hall. Now Clint knew who had sold his name to Callan, but still didn't know how the Man had gotten it. Unless Bascomb had gotten it from Nina and given it to his boss.

Clint sat on the edge of the bed, wondering how he'd managed to get himself involved with Chicago's two top crime bosses when all he wanted was to be left alone.

THIRTY-ONE

When Clint came back down to the lobby, Richard had resumed his position behind the desk. When he saw Clint, he waved him over. Clint hoped the young man wasn't going to once again thank him. The truth was Clint had almost thrown him to the wolves and cost him his job. It was only at the last minute he decided to try befriending him.

"Yeah, Richard?"

"I got a message here for you, Mr. Adams. Came in a few minutes ago." He handed Clint an envelope.

"Thanks."

Clint walked away a few feet before opening the envelope. The message was from Robert Pinkerton, asking Clint to meet him at Jackson Park.

The question was, why did Pinkerton want to meet him? And did he want to meet Pinkerton?

Clint decided out of everybody he'd met with while he'd been in Chicago, Robert Pinkerton probably wanted the least from him—so far. He decided to keep the meeting in Jackson Park, since Pinkerton had requested they meet in just an hour from now. He went out the front of the hotel, where he let the doorman get him a cab, then told the driver, "Jackson Park."

"Which part?" the man asked. "It's a big place."

"Just take me there," Clint said. "I have an hour to kill."

The driver took him to an entrance to the park. Clint decided he'd take advantage of the fact that he was early and make sure nobody was setting a trap for him.

The message Pinkerton had left told him to "Just stroll" until Pinkerton contacted him.

Once he was "strolling," he started to think this wasn't such a good idea. He was out in the open and vulnerable. What if the note hadn't been sent by Pinkerton, but by someone trying to lure him out?

After an hour, he had just about convinced himself to get out of there when suddenly, ahead of him, appeared Robert Pinkerton, wearing a suit and a bowler hat.

"Glad you made it," Pinkerton said.

"I was about to leave," Clint said. "This is very open."

"I'm sure you've checked the perimeter thoroughly," the detective said.

"Yes, I did."

"Good," Pinkerton said. "I also have a couple of men watching our backs."

"Well . . . that's comforting," Clint said.

"Come on," Pinkerton said, "let's walk. I have a favor to ask you."

"I suppose I owe you one," Clint said.

"Who knows who owes who?" Pinkerton asked. "I'll

ask this of you, and if you don't want to do it, you'll say no."

"That sounds more than fair."

Suddenly, Pinkerton fell silent.

"Well?"

"What I'm about to tell you could get a man killed," Pinkerton said.

"Oh well, take your time, then," Clint said. "Standing out here in the open can't get anybody killed."

"All right, all right," Pinkerton said. He put his hand up for Clint to stop walking, then turned to face him. "Here it is: We've got a man inside."

"Inside where?"

"Inside both men's camps," Pinkerton said. "Hughes's and Callan's."

"You've got two agents on the inside of this war?" Clint asked.

"Well," Pinkerton said, "actually, I've got one man inside both camps. The same man."

"If that's true," Clint said, "that man is playing with fire. Who do you have who's that brave—or foolish?"

"I'm going to tell you who he is because I want you to help him," Pinkerton said. "That's the favor I have to ask."

"Look, Robert," Clint said, "I'm involved with these people against my will, already. I was just in Chicago minding my own business when both of these men came at me. I'm not looking to take a hand in a war that's not mine."

"If that's the case, why haven't you just left town?" Pinkerton asked.

"I'm not ready to leave town," Clint said.

"Your ego is keeping you here," Pinkerton said. "So I thought your ego might want you to take a big part in what's going on."

"Just because I'm staying in town doesn't mean I want to get involved. What I'd really like is for everyone to leave me alone."

"Hey," Pinkerton said, "you came to me for a favor, remember?"

"All my favor required was that you answer some questions," Clint said. "I think what you're asking requires a little more than that."

"I'm asking you to help keep my man alive."

"Why should I care about your man?" Clint asked. "I don't even know him."

"Well, that's not really true."

"What?"

"You do know him."

"What are you talking ab— Oh, wait a minute," Clint said. "I haven't met that many people on both sides. Are you telling me that Carter Bascomb is a Pinkerton detective?"

"I'm telling you that, in the next few days, Carter Bascomb might end up being a dead Pinkerton detective."

THIRTY-TWO

"Wait a minute," Clint said. "I was told that Bascomb had a reputation as a criminal even before Rodney Hughes came to town."

"Who told you that?"

"A police lieutenant named Muldoon."

"Oh, him," Pinkerton said. "Well, he's trying to make a name for himself in Chicago, but in that he's right. Bascomb has been working as a crime figure in Chicago ever since we recruited him. He's helped us bring down a lot of would-be crime kings here."

"So now he's going to bring down the two top crime bosses in Chicago?"

"That's our aim," Pinkerton said, "but I'm thinking he's going to need some help."

"So why don't you send somebody in to help him?"

"Because that would take a while," Pinkerton said. "And you're already inside."

"Me? I'm not inside anything."

"You've been to see both men," Pinkerton said. "I'm

thinking they've both tried to recruit you, and that you turned them down."

"That's true."

"And since you did that, I'm thinking they both will probably try to kill you."

"I'm thinking that, too."

"Well, it seems to me you and Bascomb can help keep each other alive."

"And here I've been thinking it would be Bascomb who'd be coming for me."

"Well, one of them might try to send him, but that's when he'd have to make a decision."

"What kind of decision?"

"Kill you, or give up his secret."

"Well, I hope he makes the right choice."

"You can help him make the right choice," Pinkerton said. "He wants to reveal himself to you, but he's waiting for word from me."

"Look," Clint said, "I can't guarantee what I'll do, but give him the go-ahead, if you want."

"If he reveals himself to you, it'll be his first step toward coming out from under cover," Pinkerton said. "But the final step will be putting those two away. If we don't do that, Bascomb's as good as dead."

"Unless he stays undercover."

"He can't," Pinkerton said. "He says he's had it. He can't do it anymore."

Clint didn't like being pressured. "If Bascomb gets killed, it won't be my fault," he said. "It'll be his, for going to work for you in the first place."

"Ten years ago," Pinkerton added.

"Ten years?" Clint asked. "He's been acting a part for ten years?"

Pinkerton nodded.

"Is his name really Bascomb?"

"Yes," Pinkerton said, "we thought it would be safer for him to use his real name."

"Why don't you tell the police?" Clint asked.

"Who, Muldoon? The man's an idiot. No, I don't trust the police. They'd probably get Bascomb killed."

Clint looked around, saw some women with children walking by, and a couple of men he assumed belonged to Pinkerton.

"Okay," Clint said, "I'll talk to Bascomb about what he wants to do."

"I'll tell him," Pinkerton said. "But if you decide not to help him, I'd suggest you leave Chicago, because it's just going to get ugly."

"I'll take that under advisement."

Clint left the park before Pinkerton and his men did.

"We'll watch your back," Pinkerton told him. "Not that anyone knows we're here. We kept this meeting a total secret—unless you were followed."

"I wasn't," Clint said. "Not even by Bascomb."

Outside the park, he looked around for a passing cab, then started walking.

Pinkerton came together with his two men after Clint left the park.

"What do you think?" one of them asked.

"He'll do it," Pinkerton said.

"So our guy will be comin' out?" the other one asked. "And we'll all finally find out who this secret agent is?"

"We'll see," Pinkerton said.

"I can't imagine living undercover like that for ten years," the second man said. "I wonder what it was like."

"Maybe," Pinkerton said, "you'll be able to ask him yourself."

THIRTY-THREE

When Clint got back to the Templar, he half expected to find Bascomb already there, but in reality there probably hadn't been enough time for Pinkerton to contact him, yet.

He checked the Bull & Calf anyway, but there was no sign of the man.

He was stymied as to his next move. Sit around, nurse a beer and wait? Have lunch? No, breakfast was still lying heavy on his belly. But a walk and then lunch would give him time to think. If and when Bascomb came to him, he was going to have to already know what his course of action would be.

He left the hotel and decided to walk to Marnie's restaurant. Along the way, he considered his options. There were two that he could see: leave Chicago, or take a hand and help Bascomb. Staying and not doing anything was out of the question. He had come to that conclusion by the time he entered the small restaurant.

* * *

Jedcoe entered the outer office and leered at Nina as he always did. It made her flesh crawl.

"He's waiting for you," she said.

"What, no hello?" he asked.

His stench reached her before he did and she reared back in her chair.

"You know, you and me still got time to become really good friends," the man said to her.

She didn't know where the smell came from, his greasy hair or his black-toothed mouth. She didn't understand why Callan even did business with him, except that he always said Jedcoe was the best source of "talent."

"Go on in," she said, holding her hand up in front of her nose.

Jedcoe opened the door and entered Callan's office.

His demeanor was completely different now, as he knew not to get too close to his boss's desk.

Callan looked up, saw Jedcoe, and instinctively leaned back in his chair, but if Jedcoe kept his distance as he'd been instructed many times, Callan was usually able to avoid most of the smell. Unlike Nina, Callan knew that the smell didn't come from Jedcoe's hair or mouth, it came from him—from his body, his pores—and there didn't seem to be anything he could do about it.

"Heard you wanted to see me, Boss," Jedcoe said.

"That's right," Callan said. "I need some talent."

"Well, I'm yer guy," Jedcoe said, "you know that."

"I do know that, Jedcoe," Callan said.

"What do you need now, Boss? A woman? A thief?" Jedcoe asked.

"I need a killer, Jedcoe," Callan said. "I need a real

good, talented killer. Somebody who's not only good at it, but enjoys it, and enjoys a challenge."

"I know a few of them," Jedcoe said. "What weapon?"

"I don't care," Callan said, "but he'll have to go up against a gun. A real good gun."

"How good?" Jedcoe asked.

"Wild Bill Hickok good," Callan said. "You know, the Gunsmith good."

"That good? Ain't gonna have to draw, is he?" the smelly man asked.

"He's gonna have to do whatever he has to do," Callan said. "No limits."

"No limits," Jedcoe said, smiling. "Well, with them two words I know just the killer, Boss."

"Good," Callan said, "get him, and get out. The smell is starting to get to me."

"Yeah, Boss," Jedcoe said. "Uh, sorry. When do you want him?"

"Now!" Callan said. "I want him now, Jedcoe!"

"Comin' up, Boss," Jedcoe promised. "Comin' up."

In the outer office, Nina had produced a handkerchief, which she had scented, and was holding it in front of her face as Jedcoe came out.

"Must be somethin' big goin' on," the man said to her. "He's sure in a hurry for some specific talent."

"What kind of talent?" she asked. Bascomb would probably want to know.

"The kind that kills," Jedcoe said, "and likes it."

"Do you know somebody like that?"

"Indeed I do, missy," he said, with a black-toothed smile, "indeed I do, and I'll be bringin' him up here later today." He leaned toward her, which made her panic. "And yer gonna have to be nicer to him than you are to me."

Considering nobody else could possibly smell as bad as Jedcoe, she didn't think that would be very hard.

THIRTY-FOUR

Clint had a good meal at Marnie's, watching while she hurried from kitchen to table and back. It was a busy day for her and Matthew, and she didn't have much time to talk to Clint. He didn't mind. It gave him even more time to work out his problems.

When he was done, he paid his bill and stood to leave. She grabbed his arm as she went by.

"Can't you stay?" she asked. "I won't be busy forever."

"I'm sorry," he said. "I really have to go. I've got some things to do."

"Can you come back tonight?" she asked.

"I'll come back if I can, Marnie," he said, "but I can't promise."

"I see," she said, clearly disappointed.

"And what about Matthew?" he asked. "I think we got lucky last time he didn't hear us."

"Well," she said, "I think maybe he did hear us."

"Wha—did he say—"

"Sorry," she said. "Gotta go to work. Come back some time."

She hurried to a table, and he went out the door. The last thing he wanted to do was tangle with an irate brother, especially one the size of Matthew.

Clint realized he hadn't seen much of Chicago since he arrived. A couple of museums, a park—thanks to Robert Pinkerton—the inside of his hotel, a restaurant or two, and a couple of gangster's offices. And yet when this was over, he thought it was time for him to leave Chicago, before he got pulled into something else against his will.

When he got back to his hotel, Bascomb was waiting out front.

"Problem with the inside?" he asked, coming up next to the man.

"Yeah," Bascomb said, "there's a policeman in there."

"Looking for me?"

"I hope so," Bascomb said. "I'd hate to think he was lookin' for me."

"Muldoon?"

"Yeah."

"Let's go someplace else and talk, then."

"My thoughts, exactly."

"You know a place?"

"Yeah, but if you pick a place, nobody will be able to guess," Bascomb said, "since you don't know the city as well as I do."

"Let's take a walk," Clint said. "We'll pass something."

"Just keep in mind my appetite," Bascomb said, "that's all I ask."

Clint picked a steakhouse they walked by. It was large and did a good business, from what Clint remembered, but it wasn't their busy time yet.

"You know this place?" Clint asked.

"Yeah, but I've never been here," Bascomb admitted. "Been meaning to try it, though."

They waited until there were two huge steak dinners in front of them before they spoke.

"You talked to Pinkerton?" Bascomb asked.

"Enough to know that you're a crazy man."

"You're probably right, but what can I say? Ten years ago, I was young and wanted to make a difference."

"And now?"

"Now? Now I'm stuck. I've got to see this thing through, or the last ten years will have been wasted. Hey, this is a good steak."

Clint agreed and took another bite of his own.

"Tell me something," Clint said. "Who thinks you're working for who?"

"Wha— Oh, I see what you mean. Well, the Man thinks I'm working inside Callan's camp for him, and Callan thinks I'm working Hughes for him."

"You've got them both convinced?"

"I'm afraid so."

"You play a dangerous game."

"No more dangerous than what you play in your own backyard," Bascomb said.

"Maybe," Clint said. "How do you see this ending?"

"With both Hughes and Callan out of business and behind bars."

"You'll be satisfied with that?" Clint asked.

"Why not? They're the two biggest fish in this pond, aren't they?"

"But ten years ago, the Man didn't even exist."

"I know," Bascomb said. "I've been building a reputation all that time so that when somebody like him came along, I'd be ready."

"Callan wasn't a big enough fish for you?"

"I was ready to take care of Callan when Hughes showed up, started calling himself 'the Man,' and then started proving it. He's smart—smarter than Callan ever was."

"And what's Callan got on Hughes?"

"Nobody's meaner than him," Bascomb said. "If they were one man, he'd be unbeatable."

"Was there ever any question of them joining forces?" Clint asked.

"No," Bascomb said. "Both their egos are way too big for that."

"So when is this supposed to come to a head?" Clint asked.

"That depends on us," Bascomb said. "I can pit them against each other at any time. There's just one thing."

"What's that?"

"Callan's bringing in somebody special to take care of you," Bascomb said. "We'll have to take care of him first."

"Do you know who it is?"

"Not yet," Bascomb said, "but Callan's got a man named Jedcoe pickin' the killer out."

"Can we find Jedcoe?"

"Yes."

"How?"

"Believe me when I say," Bascomb answered, "that all we have to do is follow our noses."

"Fine," Clint said, "but let's finish our steaks first."

THIRTY-FIVE

They finished their meal just as the place started to fill up. Clint paid the bill and they went out onto the street.

"Okay, where do we find Jedcoe?" Clint asked.

"Well, we've got a couple of choices," Bascomb said. "I know where he drinks, or we can wait for him to show up at Callan's office with his man in tow."

"Is that going to happen today?"

"It should," Bascomb said. "Callan wants you taken care of right away."

"What about the Man?" Clint asked. "When is he going to send somebody after me? And when he does, will it be you?"

"It probably will be me, yeah," Bascomb said. "That's why we have to be concerned with Callan's man first."

"Okay," Clint said. "Then let's get over to his building."

"You still got that tiny little gun?" Bascomb asked.

"Yes."

"Let's make a stop along the way and get you something better."

"No argument here."

Jedcoe ordered another whiskey while he waited for his man to show up. Truthfully, if Jedcoe were not such a good judge of "talent"—whether it was whores or killers—he probably would have been the equivalent of the town drunk.

One of the only benefits of his appalling body odor was that he never had a problem getting a place at the bar. Any bar. As soon as he arrived, a spot always opened, and he was never crowded. There was a time he'd be thrown out of any bar. But when it became known that he was on John Callan's payroll, that suddenly stopped happening.

He was working on his first beer and second whiskey when a man walked in dressed in a black suit with a paisley vest. He had heavy black eyebrows over dark, hooded eyes. His expression said he'd wear any color or pattern vest that he wanted, and nobody better have anything to say about it—and nobody ever did. In fact, the man was known for his collection of brightly colored vests.

His name was Ben "the Vest" Mickelbury. He was a killer who was equally proficient with knives or guns.

The Vest spotted Jedcoe at the bar and approached him. Jedcoe didn't know how Mickelbury did it, but he never wrinkled his nose around him. It was as if he was unaware of Jedcoe's odor, which the little man appreciated.

"Word's got out already," Mickelbury said to Jedcoe.

"You wanna pull out?" Jedcoe asked.

"Get me a beer and we'll discuss it," the killer said.

Jedcoe waved to the bartender, who drew a beer, drew a breath, and held it until he set the beer down and moved away to a safe distance.

"Callan wants you in his office tonight," Jedcoe said. "We gotta go."

"No."

"Why?" Jedcoe's tone was a whine.

"Who do you think will be waitin' there for us?"

"Who?"

"Bascomb," Mickelbury said. "And from what I've been hearin', Clint Adams, the Gunsmith. You don't think he'll be waitin' there for us, too? No, we don't go to Callan's office. You go."

"Me?" Jedcoe swallowed. "But if they're waitin'—"

"They won't be waitin' for you," Mickelbury said. "That is, they won't be waitin' to kill you. They'll be waitin' to follow you."

"So what do I do?"

Mickelbury swallowed some beer, wiped his mouth with the back of his hand, and said, "You're gonna lead them right to me."

It was getting toward five o'clock and there was no sign of Jedcoe, or anyone else.

"How long does Callan stay in his office?" Clint asked Bascomb.

"Until late," Bascomb said. "He thinks nobody knows, but he also lives in this building, on the next floor up. And he keeps Nina in there until late, sometimes."

"Well, if he's waiting for Jedcoe to bring his killer, I guess we just have to wait, too."

They had picked out a doorway that was large enough to accommodate both of them, and since the building they'd chosen was abandoned, they had it all to themselves.

"Wait—" Bascomb said.

"What?"

"There he is. Jedcoe."

Clint saw a small, disheveled man walking down the block toward the building.

"That's him?"

"Yup."

"Doesn't look like the kind of man someone like Callan would count on," Clint said. "He looks like the town drunk."

"Yeah, and he smells worse. But that's him."

"And he's alone."

"I noticed," Bascomb said.

Jedcoe went into the building.

"Damn, now what?" Bascomb said.

"Now we continue to wait," Clint said. "He'll get his orders from Callan and come back down."

"And we'll follow him."

"Which is probably the plan."

"What?"

"Think about it," Clint said. "Why would Jedcoe come back here empty-handed? How will Callan react to that?"

"He'll blow his stack," Bascomb said. "And Jedcoe knows that. He wouldn't come back empty-handed unless . . ."

"Right," Clint said. "Unless that was the plan: to get us to follow Jedcoe back to the killer."

"And," Bascomb said, "back to an ambush."

"Exactly," Clint said. "Exactly."

* * *

"Mickelbury?" Callan said. "You mean, the Vest?"

"He don't like bein' called that," Jedcoe said, "but yeah, that's what they call 'im."

"If he don't like being called that, then why's he wear the damn things?" Callan demanded.

"I, uh, don't, uh—"

"Never mind," Callan said. "He's a good choice, and his plan sounds good. We'll go with it."

"So I should, uh—"

"Yeah, you should leave and let yourself be followed," Callan said. "Go! Get it done!"

"Yes, sir."

As Jedcoe hurried for the door, Callan asked, "Do you know where Bascomb is?"

"No, sir."

"All right," Callan said. "Tell my girl to come in here."

"Yes, sir."

Jedcoe went out the door. Moments later Nina Tate appeared, holding a handkerchief to her nose.

"Where's Bascomb?" he demanded.

"I don't know."

"Find him!"

She nodded and backed out.

THIRTY-SIX

Jedcoe came out of the building, hesitated, stutter-stepped, and then turned and headed back the way he had come.

"Oh yes," Bascomb said, "he knows he's going to be followed."

"Well, let's do it."

"Okay, but from this side of the street," Bascomb said. "Even if he wants to be followed, let's pretend like we don't want to be seen."

They left the doorway and started after the smelly little man.

"That gun okay?" Bascomb asked.

"It's a Peacemaker," Clint said. "It's good."

"I thought something you were more familiar with would work."

They could have gone back to Clint's hotel for his gun, but Bascomb said it was in the opposite direction.

"Listen, if this Jedcoe found somebody for this job so quickly it has to be somebody local, right?"

"Probably."

"Any guesses?"

"About who it might be?"

"Yeah," Clint said. "I'd like to have some idea of what we're walking into."

"Could be any one of three or four men," Bascomb said. "But considering it's you, somebody who's good with a gun."

"And who would that be?"

"Jesus, he's making it easy, ain't he?" Bascomb asked.

Jedcoe was walking real slow.

"Come on, Bascomb," Clint said.

"Okay, okay," Bascomb said, "it's got to be either Charlie Lawson or Ben Mickelbury."

"Mickelbury?" Clint asked.

"Yeah, but they call him the Vest."

"Why?"

"He wears black suits with colorful vests. In fact, if it's him we should be able to see his vest from a distance."

"Really? Sounds like he wouldn't last very long where I come, giving people a target like that."

"On the other hand," Bascomb said, "he's that good."

"Guess that's another way of looking at it."

They advanced a few more streets, and then Jedcoe turned left. They hurried across the street so they wouldn't lose him, but there was no danger of that. Jedcoe was still moving slow.

"Will he be alone, or bringing help?" Clint asked.

"He's probably being paid big money," Bascomb said. "He's not gonna want to share it. He'll be alone. After all, he thinks he's facing one man. And he probably thinks your reputation is inflated."

"Maybe he's right."

Bascomb looked at him, then said, "Nah, I don't think so."

About fifteen minutes later Clint said, "Okay, where's he taking us?"

"The lake," Bascomb said.

"What?"

"Lake Michigan. He's taking us down by the lake."

"So they can throw my body in when they're done?"

"Probably." Bascomb put his hand on Clint's arm, stopping. "Look, you keep following him."

"What are you going to do?"

"Circle ahead," Bascomb said. "He's moving so slow I can beat you there. Then I can spot . . . whoever it is. Lawson, Mickelbury, whoever."

"Are you sure?"

"Yeah, I'm sure," Bascomb said. "He's taking us to the lake."

"Okay," Clint said.

"Yeah?" Bascomb said.

"Yeah," Clint said. "Go."

THIRTY-SEVEN

The lake suddenly stretched out in front of Clint.

Jedcoe was walking down a hill. Clint stopped. He figured the base of the hill was the spot. It was getting on toward dusk and there was no sun to speak of.

When he started down the hill, he saw three men at the bottom—Jedcoe, Bascomb, and a man wearing a black suit and red and yellow vest. When he got close enough, he saw the vest was yellow flowers on a red background.

"See?" the Vest said to Bascomb. "No ambush. I was gonna do this man to man. But I guess now it's two against one?"

Bascomb looked at Clint, who shook his head.

"No," Bascomb said, "I just wanted to make sure. Come on, Jedcoe. Get out of the way before you catch a stray bullet."

Jedcoe started toward him.

"Christ, no, don't come near me!" Bascomb said. "Go the other way, downwind."

Unfazed, Jedcoe changed direction.

"You Adams?" Mickelbury asked.

"That's right."

"No holster?"

"I don't wear a holster when I'm in a city," Clint said.

"I do," Mickelbury said. He opened his jacket, exhibiting a shoulder rig.

"Whatever you need to do," Clint said. He had the Peacemaker stuck in his belt in front, just to the left, for a cross draw.

"You mind if I take off my jacket?" Mickelbury asked.

"Like I said," Clint answered, "whatever you've got to do."

Mickelbury took off his jacket, tossed it away.

"I hope the vest doesn't blind you," he said.

"No you don't," Clint said.

Mickelbury laughed, then moved. He was incredibly fast. His gun cleared leather as Clint pulled the trigger. Clint's bullet went right through the yellow flower on Mickelbury's heart. More red blossomed. Mickelbury had a shocked look on his face. His gun dropped from his hand and he looked down at his chest. With both hands, he felt his chest until he found the blood.

"Sonofa—" he started, and then fell facedown in the sand.

"Jesus," Jedcoe said.

"Go and tell Callan what you saw, Jedcoe," Bascomb said.

"You want him to tell Callan he saw you here?" Clint asked.

"Why not?" Bascomb asked. "It's time to tie this all up."

"You ain't gonna kill me?" Jedcoe asked.

"If we did, we'd be doing the city of Chicago a favor," Bascomb said. "But not yet. Maybe later. Go."

Jedcoe started running.

"He's gonna come after us with everything he's got," Bascomb said.

"That bother you?"

"It would have, any other time," Bascomb said. "I never had anybody I thought could stand with me."

"Well," Clint said, "I think I'd like to go back to my hotel and get my own gun."

"Now?"

"Oh yeah," Clint said, tossing the borrowed gun to Bascomb. "This one pulls a little to the left."

THIRTY-EIGHT

When Clint and Bascomb returned to Clint's hotel, they went straight to his room. Clint strapped on his gun belt, then donned his jacket, which almost hid it. When they came back down, they saw Nina Tate in a heated argument with Richard, the desk clerk.

"I can't let you up there, ma'am," Richard was saying. "I could get fired, this time."

"Nina!" Bascomb called.

She turned and looked relieved when she saw him.

"Oh my God." She threw her arms around him. "He wanted me to find you, and when I couldn't he got very angry. Then that smelly man came in and said that you and Clint Adams had killed Mickelbury—"

"Actually, Clint did that alone."

"It doesn't matter," she said. "He wants you both dead. I rushed out to warn you, but I could only think to come here."

"It's okay," Bascomb said. "Go home, Nina. Don't go back to the office. You're through working there."

"What are you going to do?"

"Finish this."

She looked at Clint.

"Will you help him?"

"Yes," Clint answered. "Do as he says and go home."

"Stay there until I come for you. Understand?" Bascomb asked.

"Yes."

She kissed him, and they walked her out and put her in a cab.

"How do you want to play this?" Clint asked.

"Well, we could wait for them to come for us, or—"

"—we could take the fight to them."

"Right."

"Who first?"

"Callan," Bascomb said. "If we take him first, Hughes will think I did it because I'm working for him. Then we'll be able to take him."

"Take 'em both right where they live?" Clint asked.

"Why not?" Bascomb said. "If we keep it off the street, the police won't get involved, and we can avoid any kind of ambush."

"They won't expect it?" Clint asked.

"I don't think so."

"How many men does Callan keep in his building?"

"I'm not sure," Bascomb said. "He keeps them out of his office. I've only ever seen two of them."

"Maybe the two I saw," Clint said. "What about hitting Pinkerton for more help?"

"That'll just give Callan time to collect more men," Bascomb said. "We have to go and do it now."

"All right, then," Clint said. "We better get going."

THIRTY-NINE

They went back to Callan's building and entered by the front door, guns drawn. They did not encounter any resistance there.

"They must all be upstairs," Bascomb said.

"If they figure we're coming, they'll be waiting," Clint said. "Is there a back way?"

"Yeah, there is. This hall goes all the way to a back door. There's a stairway there."

"You want the front or the back?" Clint asked.

"Well, since this is my game and you're just backing me up, I'll take the front."

"Give me five minutes, then start up," Clint said.

"Right. Good luck."

"You, too."

"And Clint?"

"Yeah?"

"Thanks."

"Thank me after," Clint said.

"I'd rather do it now, while I'm still alive," Bascomb said.

Clint nodded, and they split up.

Clint moved down the hallway and found the stairwell. He moved slowly up the stairs to the floor where Callan's office was. Bascomb had told him Callan lived one level above that, but they were going to try his office first.

The back stairs brought him into the hallway at the opposite end from where Callan's office was. Bascomb was already ahead of him, approaching the office door. Clint stayed behind the man to watch his back.

Bascomb reached the office door and opened it as silently as he could. He stuck his head in, and Clint saw his shoulders slump from behind.

Clint came up behind him and said, "What is it?"

"Empty," Bascomb said. "And the door to Callan's office is open. It's never open. Means he ain't there."

They moved into the outer office to check and found they were right. Callan's office was empty.

"Upstairs?" Clint asked.

"Gotta be."

"What's the setup?"

"No offices, it's all an open living space."

"No place for us to hide."

"No," Bascomb said, "but the same is true of him."

"I'll take the back again?"

Bascomb shook his head.

"The back stairway is blocked up there. Only one way in and one way out."

"Is there access from outside?"

"No."

"Okay, then," Clint said. "Guess that makes our decision easy."

"Yup."

They headed for the main stairway and went up.

"What do you hear?" Clint asked Bascomb, who was ahead of him on the stairway.

"Nothing."

Clint looked down. Nobody was coming up behind them.

"We just gotta go through the door," Bascomb said.

"Okay," Clint said. "I'll follow you in."

"Thanks."

There was no door. If it was an ambush, it was a quiet one.

Bascomb took a deep breath and charged through the door. When he was on a level part of the floor, he threw himself down and rolled.

Clint followed him through, hit the floor, and rolled in the opposite direction. They both came up with their guns drawn.

The large room, which ran the length of the building, was empty. There was furniture, but nothing large enough for a man of Callan's size to hide behind. And there were no other men.

"He cleared out," Bascomb said.

"Why would he do that?" Clint asked. "He's not afraid, is he?"

"Not the type to be afraid," Bascomb said.

"So what's next?"

Bascomb looked at Clint.

"They could be waiting for us outside."

"Or?"

"Or he could've taken some men and went after Nina, to use her as a hostage."

"He knows about you and Nina?"

"I didn't think so," Bascomb said, "but he might."

"I guess we better find out, then."

FORTY

They made their way back down to the lobby.

"We could end up in a shoot-out on the street, after all," Bascomb said.

"And they'd probably have the back covered," Clint said.

"Might as well go out the front, then."

"Agreed."

They drew their guns and, together, walked out the front door.

Jedcoe cringed when Slater opened the door to the Man's office.

"Oh, what the hell—" Slater said, fanning the air.

"I got a message for the Man," Jedcoe said.

"From who?" Slater asked.

"Mr. Callan."

"Jesus," Slater said, "well, you ain't comin' in here smellin' like that. Just wait in the hall."

He slammed the door in Jedcoe's face and walked through to his boss's inner office.

"What is it?" the Man demanded as Slater knocked.

"Callan has sent a message with that smelly Jedcoe," Slater said.

"Christ, you didn't let him in, did you?"

"No, he's out in the hall."

The Man shook his head, but stood up from his desk and followed Slater to the door.

"Open the door," the Man said.

Jedcoe was startled as the door opened, which, if anything, increased his body odor.

"Let's hear it, and make it fast," the Man said.

"Mr. Callan said he thought you'd be interested to know that your man Bascomb is a Pinkerton agent."

"What?"

Jedcoe kept going quickly. "He said Bascomb's been workin' in both your camps, and now he's joined forces with the Gunsmith. They killed Ben Mickelbury today."

"How do I know you're telling the truth?" the Man asked.

"Mister," Jedcoe said, "I'm just too scared to lie."

The Man looked at Slater. "If this is true," he said, "looks like you're going to get your chance to kill Bascomb."

"Mr. Callan says you and him should join forces against Bascomb and the Gunsmith."

"Is that a fact?"

"H-He wants me to bring him your answer."

The Man looked at Slater. "Give him my answer, Slater."

Jedcoe looked at Slater just as the big man shoved a

large knife through his belly. The odor that followed was like an explosion.

"Oh, Jesus!" the Man said. "Get the body out of here. Deliver it to Callan."

"But . . . where is Callan?" Slater asked. "We, uh, killed Jedcoe before he could tell us."

When the Man realized Slater was right, he scowled and said, "Fuck."

Clint and Bascomb looked up and down the street, across the way, and up at the rooftops.

"Nothing," Bascomb said. "Nobody. What's going on?"

"Maybe," Clint said, "we're not so much in the minds of these men as we think."

"Whaddaya mean?"

"Maybe they're concerned with somebody else."

"Like Nina?"

"No," Clint said, "like each other."

FORTY-ONE

It took them twenty minutes to get from Callan's building to the Man's building.

"What's the difference here?" Clint asked.

"The difference is the Man owns the entire building," Bascomb said, "while Callan simply rents two floors of the building he's in."

"So, can we use the roof to get in?"

"Oh yeah," Bascomb said, "we can definitely use the roof—but we need to get to the rooftop next to it."

"Sounds like you've scouted it already," Clint commented.

"Well, yeah," Bascomb said, "I mean, I figured just in case. You know?"

"I know," Clint said. "Lead the way."

Clint followed Bascomb to the building next to the Man's. It wasn't locked, so they went inside, and he trailed Bascomb up the stairs to the roof, which was about one story higher than the building they were interested in.

"Now what?" Clint asked.

"Now we jump."

"What?"

"We jump."

"You jump," Clint said. "I'll go back down and use the front door."

"Come on, it's not that far," Bascomb said.

"It's far, and a long way down," Clint said.

"Don't tell me you've never jumped rooftops in the West," Bascomb said. "We do it all the time in Chicago."

"Any rooftop jumping I may have done I did in my youth," Clint said. "I broke my leg once—and I was more flexible then."

"Just bend your knees when you land," Bascomb said.

Slater opened the door and was surprised to see John Callan there with some men behind him. In fact, he had a hard time seeing the men behind Callan because the man was so big. But Slater was a big man, too.

"Tell your boss I'm here," Callan said.

"Wait a minute—"

Slater had put his hand out to keep Callan from entering. Callan reached out and took the man's hand. They stared at each other, muscles flexing. Slater felt in control, but suddenly his confidence waned as he felt John Callan exert pressure. The big man's strength was amazing.

"Now, you want a broken hand, or you want to go and tell your boss I'm here?" Callan asked.

"I'll tell him," Slater said, gritting his teeth.

Callan released his hand. Slater flexed it to see if any fingers were broken. Callan entered, five men coming in behind him.

"We'll wait here, out of respect," Callan told Slater. "But we won't wait long."

"I'll tell him."

Slater turned and walked away.

"Who?" the Man demanded.

"Callan."

"At my door?"

"Inside."

"Any men?"

"Five."

"How many we got in the building?"

"Three."

The Man opened his top drawer, took out his gun, and shoved it into his belt.

"All right, let's go see what he wants," the Man said, "but if I give the word, you kill him."

"Mr. Callan?"

"That's right," the Man said. "Is that a problem?"

"Uh, no," Slater said, "no problem."

"Let's go."

Clint watched as Bascomb jumped. The man bent his knees, rolled, and came up with his arms spread. The only thing missing was him yelling "Ta-da!"

"Come on," Bascomb called. "It's easy."

"Easy," Clint said to himself.

He jumped.

The Man came down the hall, watching Callan and his men carefully.

"Can't have a shoot-out in this hall, Hughes," Callan said. "Take your hand off your gun."

"Don't call me that," the Man said.

"Call you what? Your name?"

"What do you and your men want?"

"Bascomb," Callan said. "He and Clint Adams are on their way. We need to take care of them."

"Isn't Bascomb your man?" the Man asked.

"He's been my man, your man, who else's man? The police? The Pinkertons? And now he's got the Gunsmith helping him. Adams killed Ben Mickelbury in a fair fight. You know how good he had to be to do that?"

"Mickelbury was good," the Man admitted.

"If they went to my building, they found it empty. That means they're on their way here. You got men in the building?"

"You know I do."

"You, me, our men, we can take Bascomb and Adams."

"And then what?"

"And then we go back to business as usual," Callan said. "Tryin' to cut each other's throats."

"So you're proposing a truce?"

"I'm proposing we work together for, what? An hour? However long it takes us to kill two men."

The Man thought it over, then turned to Slater.

"Okay, get the other men, bring them in here," he said.

"We workin' together?" Slater asked.

The Man nodded.

FORTY-TWO

"Locked," Bascomb said.

"There's no hatch?" Clint asked.

"Just this door."

Bascomb pulled on the door again, but it didn't budge.

"Now what do we do?" Clint asked. "Jump back up?"

"I never learned how to jump back up," Bascomb said.

Clint walked to the edge of the roof and looked down in time to see some men going into the building.

"I don't think we're going to have to try," he said.

"Why?"

He turned to face Bascomb.

"I think somebody's going to be opening the door for us."

"Is that right?" Bascomb asked. "Then I guess we better get ready."

"Yeah," Clint said, looking around for cover. There was none, except to stand to either side of the door.

"If we get them coming out the door, we can have them in a cross fire," Clint said.

"That's okay with me," Bascomb said.

At that point, they heard somebody trying the doorknob. Clint ducked to the right, while Bascomb stood off to the left of the door.

The door opened and three men with guns came rushing out, looking around the roof.

"Hey!" Clint yelled, not wanting to shoot them in the back.

All three men turned and their eyes widened when they saw Clint and Bascomb, who wasted no time in firing. A couple of the men squeezed off useless shots that went into the roof. In seconds, though, the three men were dead.

Bascomb moved in to walk among them and take a look.

"Uh-oh," he said.

"What?"

"That one works for the Man," he said, "and those two work for Callan." He looked at Clint. "Seems like they joined up against us."

"You ever figure that would happen?"

"Didn't think so," Bascomb said. "I thought they hated each other too much."

"Maybe," Clint said, "they hate you even more, for fooling them both."

"Maybe," Bascomb said. "Well, anyway, the door's open."

"And we have extra guns."

They each picked up an extra pistol and ammo and shoved them into belts and pockets.

"I'll go first," Bascomb said. "Still my party."

"I'm with you."

They entered the stairwell slowly at first, then took the stairs more quickly.

"Where are we?" Clint asked.

"This is the floor the Man has his office on."

Bascomb stepped into the hall. Immediately, there were shots. He drew back.

"Two men, end of the hall," he said to Clint.

At that moment Clint heard something.

"We've got two, maybe three men coming up from downstairs," he said.

"Nowhere to go," Bascomb said.

"If you keep the two at the end of the hall pinned down so they can't charge us, I'll handle the ones coming up the stairs."

"Okay."

Bascomb drew the second gun and, with a gun in each hand, stepped into the hall and began to fire.

Clint also palmed a second gun, turned to face the men coming up the stairs. He had an advantage, in that he knew they were coming. When they appeared, he simply began to fire. Taken by surprise, the three men fired off some ineffectual shots as Clint's bullets struck home. They all tumbled back down the stairs, dead.

He turned to Bascomb, who had stopped firing.

"Pin them down?" he asked.

"Better than that," Bascomb said. "Killed 'em."

"The hall's empty?"

"Yeah, but they might be trying to draw us in."

"What choice do we have?"

They ejected the spent shells from their guns and reloaded.

"All right," Clint said. "It's the door at the end, right?"

"That's right."

"Any other ways in?"

"No," Bascomb said, "but that means there are no other ways out, either."

"Let's go, then," Clint said. "This time together."

Bascomb nodded and they stepped into the hall.

FORTY-THREE

"Slater," the Man said, "check the hall."

"Take these two with you," Callan said.

Slater was hesitant, but left the Man's office with two of Callan's men. That left Callan and the Man alone.

"No shots for a few minutes," Callan said.

"You think they're dead?"

"I hope not," Callan said. "I want to kill that bastard Bascomb myself."

"And Adams?"

"You can have him."

The Man stood up and looked out the window.

"What do you see?" Callan asked.

"I see you," the Man said. "Dead." He turned and shot Callan in the chest.

Clint and Bascomb were about to kick the door in when they heard movement on the other side. They had no place to go, so they just stepped back and waited.

The door opened and two gunmen stood in the doorway. Before they could draw, Clint and Bascomb shot them down. Slater stood behind the two men, startled and frozen.

"Don't," he said to Bascomb.

"Drop your knife," Bascomb said.

Slater took his knife out and dropped it to the ground.

"No gun?" Clint asked.

"Slater doesn't carry a gun," Bascomb said.

"What do you want to do with him?" Clint asked.

Bascomb hesitated just a few seconds and then said, "Let him go."

"What?" Clint said.

"What?" Slater echoed.

"Let him go," Bascomb said, again. "It's all over, anyway."

Clint stepped aside and said, "Go!"

"Really?" Slater asked, looking at Bascomb.

"Really."

"You ain't gonna shoot me in the back?"

"Go! Before I change my mind," Bascomb said.

Slater rushed past them, then said, "There was a shot from the office just now."

"Who's in there?" Bascomb asked.

"Just Callan and the Man."

"Okay, go."

Slater ran down the hall.

"The office," Bascomb said, and led the way.

The bullet struck Callan in the chest as he was standing up. It had been his intention to kill the Man while he was looking, but the Man was quicker.

Or so he thought.

The bullet didn't slow Callan down and the Man didn't have time to pull the trigger again . . .

As Clint and Bascomb came to the office door, they saw Callan's broad back. It looked like the man was bent over something—or someone.

"Stand aside, Callan!" Bascomb shouted. "Hands up."

Callan stopped what he was doing and turned. The front of his shirt was stained red.

"The sonofabitch shot me," he said. "I had to kill him before this bullet kills me."

As he stepped aside, Callan released the Man's lifeless body, which fell to the floor. Callan had choked him to death.

Callan staggered, reached out for support, missed the desk, and fell to his knees. Clint could see that he had been shot in the chest, around the heart.

"Damn it," he said. "Damn you, Bascomb."

As Callan fell onto his face, Bascomb said, "Just doing my job."

Clint and Bascomb stepped out onto the street. The building was strewn with dead bodies, including Jedcoe, who they found in a closet.

"I'll have to get the police over here," Bascomb said, "and report to my boss."

"Then what?"

"On to my next job."

"You going to be somebody else again for ten years?" Clint asked.

"No," Bascomb said, "I think I'll be myself for a

while. Why don't you get out of here? The police will probably keep you and question you for hours."

"You sure you don't need me?"

"Hey," Bascomb said, "the hard part is over."

Clint shrugged and said, "Okay."

"You could buy me another meal tomorrow," Bascomb said, "for old time's sake."

"Make it breakfast at my hotel," Clint said. "And after that I'm getting on a train."

"Leaving Chicago?"

"Oh yeah," Clint said, "time to get back to where I know all the players."

Watch for

SHOWDOWN IN CHEYENNE

348th novel in the exciting GUNSMITH series from Jove

Coming in December!

And don't miss

ANDERSONVILLE VENGEANCE

Gunsmith Giant Edition 2010

Available from Jove in November!

GIANT ACTION! GIANT ADVENTURE!

THE GUNSMITH

J.R. ROBERTS

Little Sureshot And
The Wild West Show
(Gunsmith Giant #9)

Dead Weight
(Gunsmith Giant #10)

Red Mountain
(Gunsmith Giant #11)

The Knights of Misery
(Gunsmith Giant #12)

The Marshal from Paris
(Gunsmith Giant #13)

Lincoln's Revenge
(Gunsmith Giant #14)

Andersonville Vengeance
(Gunsmith Giant #15)

penguin.com/actionwesterns

GIANT-SIZED ADVENTURE FROM AVENGING ANGEL LONGARM.

BY TABOR EVANS

2006 Giant Edition:
LONGARM AND THE OUTLAW EMPRESS

2007 Giant Edition:
LONGARM AND THE GOLDEN EAGLE SHOOT-OUT

2008 Giant Edition:
LONGARM AND THE VALLEY OF SKULLS

2009 Giant Edition:
LONGARM AND THE LONE STAR TRACKDOWN

2010 Giant Edition:
LONGARM AND THE RAILROAD WAR

penguin.com/actionwesterns

DON'T MISS A YEAR OF

Slocum Giant
by
Jake Logan

**Slocum Giant 2004:
Slocum in the Secret Service**

**Slocum Giant 2005:
Slocum and the Larcenous Lady**

**Slocum Giant 2006:
Slocum and the Hanging Horse**

**Slocum Giant 2007:
Slocum and the Celestial Bones**

**Slocum Giant 2008:
Slocum and the Town Killers**

**Slocum Giant 2009:
Slocum's Great Race**

**Slocum Giant 2010:
Slocum Along Rotten Row**

penguin.com/actionwesterns